Thomas Mark Casey. My mate, Slough RFC grandee and all-round bally top bloke. Cheers for your rugby and gag brain. We will co-write and co-produce the TV series.

1

The two pitches at Badcock Town RFC resembled something from the Somme at the end of WW1. After two weeks of solid rain, the green from the grass disappeared into the dark brown from the mud. Luckily though, no deluge was spoiling this occasion. All players, coaching, social and managerial staff were standing in one half of pitch number 1. They were all in suits to varying degrees of sartorial elegance, a few of them only ever wore one when appearing in court. Ashley Havers and Howley Davies were rooted on halfway, facing the ensemble. The former was the club's new owner looking the business in an immaculate black suit, white shirt and black tie. His £300, highly polished Loake brogues sank in the quagmire, making him wince at the rot being caused to such expensive footwear. Howley had spiky, dyed blonde hair (a man with more lines on his face than Nazca, would not have a naturally golden barnet) and was as unkempt as his crumpled old suit. Underneath the jacket, he wore a 70s Wales rugby replica top. His shoes were already muddy and ruined because they were his twenty-year-old rugby boots. Ashley was holding an urn and addressing everyone.

"So as the former chairman, and total club legend..." he enthused. The gathering nodded and a few shouted 'Jocks!' A swirling gust of wind caught Howley's eye. Unseen by Ashley, the coach moved three steps to the side away from him. "Jockey wanted his ashes sprinkled on this very sacred ground." Ashley took the top off the urn and tipped out its contents. The squall changed direction entirely, it was the *Badcock Fart*. Thanks to the geography of the pitch, the positioning of the clubhouse and a steep hill on the far side of the complex, a tornado-like phenomenon occurred when certain conditions existed. It had caused opposing kickers problems in the past, creating mayhem when it struck. It was never enough to help the team win though and only served to make the opposition miss a few kicks. Winning was not in BTRFC's DNA. The ashes hovered in the air magically as one cloud. The fart did its thing, changed direction again, picked them up in a swirling mass and deposited them all over the speaker, covering him from head-to-toe in Jockey. Ashley stood motionless in disbelief. Howley let out a deep sigh and looked to the sky.

"Just had one fucking job," he muttered whilst moving up to face Ashley. He looked the owner in the eye and then averted his gaze down to address the front of his now grey/white/black suit. "It's your round when I get up there big lad," he said, shuffled off with a slight limp behind Ashley and headed for the clubhouse where the beer lived. Havers was still motionless. David Hamilton was next to move up. Upright, square shoulders, blazer, shirt and tie, a para serviceman beret and a long line of medals pinned across his barrel of a chest. He marched up swinging his arms as if on parade and when he reached Ashley, did the double feet stomp action a soldier does when they come to a halt. He saluted briskly.

"Pleasure serving under you sir," He paused, still holding his pose, staring in the distance as though he'd spotted a sniper on the horizon. There was a hint of his lower jaw quivering. This was followed by a dramatic dispatch of the hand which returned sharply to his side. He did the soldier's turn away and marched again, off after Howley. The rest of the gathering matched them, filing past Ashley en masse, paying their respects to the deceased as they passed by.

"Shall we call Ghostbusters?" quipped one to no reaction from the target of the jibe. Ashley had to take the suit, and Jockey, to a specialist cleaner to extract as much of the departed chairman as they could. He had no idea where to look, but the funeral directors pointed him towards 'Magic & Sons'. These masters of the scrub also specialised in sorting the cabs after inebriated punters had deposited their insides over the back seat. Normal soap and water didn't cut the mustard as all it would do is create an odour akin to a dead person. Once the surface of the offending vomit had been scraped away, they employed a hoover that captured the tiny particles that cause the smell. It is this bit of kit they used to get as much of Jockey as possible out of the suit. Surprisingly they managed to find at least half of him and empty it into another urn. Ashley later revisited the ceremony to deposit Jockey on the pitch, this time on his own.

It was quite a turn of events that led to Ashley, who knew nothing whatsoever about rugby, becoming the new owner and chairman of Badcock Town RFC.

2

Ashley opened the boardroom door at Smythe & Sons, a solicitor's office in Badcock Town high street.

"Zippy!" shouted Julian Watson, one of four sitting around the table. He got this nickname after an incident at his old university's TV channel. The station was broadcast on the uni's Facebook page. The studio helped media studies students pretend they were getting real TV experience. As a former undergraduate, Ashley had been invited on their live chat show to discuss the success alumni could expect after obtaining a degree. Once the programme was over, he vanished off to the toilet still wearing his radio microphone. Because no one in the studio knew what they were doing and the sound guy was outside having a smoke, the mic was happily broadcasting his peeing and breaking wind live across the airwaves. This wasn't the embarrassing bit for Ashley though. When finished, he caught his foreskin in the zipper and screamed like someone who'd been shot and stumbled around the toilet, swearing incoherently. The channel was mistakenly still on the air, and he burst into the studio squealing for help. A student cameraman decided to focus on Ashley's groin area, now occupied by half his bloody penis hanging out the front of his trousers. Eventually, a grown-up found the off switch and called an ambulance. Of course the video was a big hit across socials.

Julian was in his early forties, but excessive drinking had taken its toll on his face which bore a striking resemblance to a shiny plum. It wasn't just the grog that he did to unhealthy extremes. His terrible diet meant his heart screamed audibly as it strained to push blood around his enormous mass. The other factor in his lifestyle that had undertakers measuring him up for a big coffin, was the complete lack of physical exercise. Even the slight aerobic benefit gained from masturbating had stopped when he couldn't reach it anymore.

He was also batshit crazy, genuinely believing that aliens created our planet and existed amongst us in human form. They amused themselves by coming up with ways to irritate the utter shite out of mankind. Some examples were: politicians, balsamic reduction, Youtubers, reality TV stars, wokeness, people getting into lifts before letting others out and those that listened to stuff loudly on tinny phone speakers. His list was endless and formed of anything that drove him to despair. This included PR consultants, Ashley's profession. Despite that, Havers liked him, he was always fun even when things weren't, an exceptionally good trait to have in life. They'd had serious nights on the pop over the years which meant Julian consumed pretty much all of his companion's contribution to the occasions. Ashley wasn't known for his capability to handle alcohol. The total opposite in fact, a notoriously bad drinker, he had the constitution of a gnat.

He was at Smythe & Sons for the reading of his godfather's will. John Weir (aka Jockey) died after a heart attack whilst in frantic action with a prostitute called Madam Cyn in a BDSM dungeon. The cardiac condition and the dominatrix were news to his ex-second wife. She refused to come to the solicitor's let alone the cremation. In her eyes, it was just a massive embarrassment. His children: Sarah (youngest), Nicola (middle), and Julian (oldest) all took his demise in different ways. Julian found humour in the situation, he never liked his step-mum, and it gave him one hell of a story to tell at parties. Nicola, stunning but a blancmange for a personality, was hugely unmoved by the whole thing. Sarah, AKA the black widow, was the half-sister, her mum being Jockey's second wife. There was a 16-year age gap between her and Julian. She bore all the traits of her mum rather than her father.

"Christ, what you are you doing here?" hissed Sarah.

"Mr Weir requested it," said the solicitor, whose demeanour suggested he was not all that happy with his lot.

"God knows why," she spat. Ashley didn't understand why too. He hadn't been especially close to him and in fact, hardly ever saw this appointed guardian.

Havers had what he saw as an ideal childhood. His parents emigrated to the Philippines before he was a glint in their eyes. Dad, an accountant, found lucrative work in the South Asian country. He and he and his fiancée upped sticks to live there. When Ashley came along, they wanted to make sure he got a good education and packed him off to boarding school in England, only to return on holidays. The reason this stood for an ideal was that his best pal in the Philippines, Josh, had also been sent to the same place - the parents were good friends. They had a rare old time at school and when term broke up, both returned to their family's bosom where they did everything kids do on vacation together. The tropical weather, even in the rainy summer months, meant it was still very warm, allowing for a large outdoor playground. This was especially true when they were teenagers and the beach was somewhere to spot, and fail miserably at, chatting up girls.

Ashley's father, Nigel, and Jockey became friends at uni. The Scot hailed from Govan, the hard-as-nails area of Glasgow. Nigel from Surrey where the only hard thing was the granite work surfaces in many of the local kitchens. They both went through college together studying accountancy. Havers Snr was tall gangly and accident-prone. Jockey had been mined from rock with a blunt pick. They had different skill sets and so played different sports. Dad - badminton, Jockey - a formidable No 8 with fists like JCBs and a face that had been bashed up so many times, it resembled Bagpuss. The nights out post-matches were poles apart but both tried to attend the other's shindigs.

After getting their degrees, both joined different firms to qualify fully as accountants. Jockey by this stage was playing for the Scottish international side. In that pre-professional era, all test rugby players had normal jobs. It was the days when the second rows were usually policemen. The boys-in-blue (as it was then) recruitment policy was to get the biggest guys possible.

With the lack of guns, you could always rely on a 6ft 8in copper nicknamed the Blackpool Tower. They'd not just scare a criminal but maybe give them a clip round the ear whilst apprehending said miscreant. Baxter & Baxter practically bit his hand off to join them. They were ex-pats who favoured the wealthier clients from north of the border that had settled in the south of England. With Jockey as 'their guy', they hoovered up every England-based Scottish client available to the accountancy world. All of this meant that he didn't have to do much work, training and international duty saw to that. He was hardly at his desk, but the firm took that as an excellent trade-off. If anyone called to make an appointment with him (which they did frequently) he held an 'open day' where all the meetings were knocked off all in one go allowing him to get back to his sport for the rest of the month. Baxter & Baxter's marketing policy was based on inviting clients and future clients to the rugby. They all had a wonderful day and went home with the story that the Scottish number 8 was their accountant.

It was the opposite case for Nigel who ended up at a big US firm with branches all around the world. They wanted their pound of flesh, so the limited spare time didn't allow him to play much badminton. He had a few matches a month for his local club, but even that stopped when work pressures became greater. It was this firm that offered him the position in the Philippines. When the Havers' made their decision to stay in Southeast Asia after Ashley was born, there was only one person to ask to be his godfather - the big yin.

Sarah was an out-and-out hard ass. Her first husband, a teetotal parish councillor, passed away in suspicious circumstances after consuming a form of rat poison. No hard evidence was found that linked his wife to the doomed ingestion but that didn't stop all the village gossip. Her second husband died in a car crash after he drove home from the pub on their Gloucestershire farm. They hadn't gotten on for years. Once the kids had left for uni, the relationship deteriorated until they'd rather have had root canal surgery than spend time in each other's company. So he would disappear down the local pub at the end of the lane and drive home when he couldn't even walk. On the fateful night, being blotto, he first got into the wrong car. Not hard considering many same-coloured Land Rovers were awaiting their owners. After finally getting the right one, he headed back. The pub car park and the lane were all on private land, so he broke no laws nor endangered any other road users on his nightly return to the homestead. As he rounded a corner, a deer ran out in front of the car. Having a blood alcohol level as if he were a bottle of surgical spirit, the car behaved like a knob of butter sliding down a hot pan. He yanked the steering wheel right, just missed the deer but had no ability to influence the motor now careering through the hedge. He hit a horse before the tree that killed him. Sarah never forgave him, the nag was her favourite animal in the world, and she loved it like it was one of her children. Again village gossip laid the blame at Sarah's door. She could hardly have been accountable for an action by an idiot who could've just walked home, meaning the horse and him stayed alive, but that didn't stop them.

The reading progressed uneventfully with no surprises. The solicitor didn't judge the room properly however. The family all just wanted to know how much loot they were in for and had their trainers laced, but he dragged it out as though he was avoiding going home. The children all got a fair share, as did the first wife, but nothing for the second wife who had already received a big settlement in the divorce.

"There's just one item remaining," the lawyer said stopping all gathering their things and bolting for the exit. "To my dear godson Ashley, I leave Badcock Town RFC." The statement was greeted with stony silence. Everyone looked around at each other with a shrug.

"Bloody bad luck Zippy," Julian bellowed.

"What's that?" Ashley asked.

"His poxy rugby club," said Sarah.

"An utterly crap rugby club with a truly awful team. It was dad's life for some godforsaken reason," Julian was liking this story.

"You're welcome to it," Sarah said.

3

Ashley's Brazilian wife, Thais, was waiting in the driver's seat of their Mercedes as he appeared from the solicitor's office.

"So?" she asked. Ashley was sure the accent got stronger and her grammar worse each year.

"It seems I've been given a rugby club."

"What?"

"A rugby club."

"Money?"

"That went to his kids, rightly."

"You know nothing rugby."

"Let alone running a club," Ashley agreed.

"We sell."

"Ah, bit of a problem with that."

"No problem, Hans sell."

"Ohh yes, of course, mister perfect hair can sort it out," Ashley sniffed. Thais started the car.

"Quicker better," she said as they moved off.

"He'll have to wait."

"He no good to wait."

"Tough titty. I, as the owner, not you, can't sell until the end of a season.

"How long is?"

"No idea, Sarah's going to give me a heads up."

"Ah, black widow love that."

"I don't know why you're so down on her."

"Girl thing."

"You've always had something against her. You like Julian and Nicola but for no reason whatsoever, you hate Sarah."

"Around her, you like puppy dog with lipstick out."

"Not this again."

They met in her hometown of Rio when one of his clients moved there. Ashley found the city totally intoxicating. First, there really was samba in the air. They loved to party, have a great time and flash their pearly whites in big, wonderful smiles at every opportunity. There were of course the beaches, not just the famous Copacabana or Ipanema but plenty of astounding other less well-known spots with white sand and warm sea. Yes, the favelas were not places to visit but nor were some of the run-down areas in London, although you were more likely to be killed in a favela than the Wetwang Estate in Peckham - just. Then, there were the women, oh the women. He fell in love every corner he turned. Tanned, dark hair, dark eyes and curves in all the right places. He noticed that as a Brazilian woman, it was highly likely you'd be partial to wearing a dental floss bikini, no matter the wearer's age, shape, or size. This was fine by him. He had a fun time romantically but then fell in love, at first sight. They were introduced at a party given by his client, she took his breath away. Tall (like him) hair in a ponytail, eyes that melted his soul and a smile he would follow into Hades. This first encounter didn't go well though.

"It's pronounced thaa-ees," she explained clearly having been asked so many times by non-Brazilians.

"Ah, mine is pronounced ashhh-leeee."

"I know," she said with a raised eyebrow and look as though she'd just trodden in something "Could you help me out." Her accent melted his heart.

"Sure, which way did you come in?" As soon as he said it, the ground needed to swallow him up. She was so beautiful, composed, confident, and classy, she made him nervous and self-conscious. The result was terrible jokes. Thais looked at him puzzled as if she regretted getting the short straw in him.

"Do English eat jellied eels and mushy peas?"

"Oh, they're the EastEnders."

"The who?"

"You know, pearly kings and queens." She looked completely bemused. Cue the mockney accent. "That dental flosser is proper elephant's trunk," She had no idea what he was talking about but that didn't stop him. "He's a Berkeley Hunt and right barney rubble." He knew these because of a college game where the winner had to know the rudest cockney rhyming slang. The Berkeley one won him a round. Thais moved off like there was a nauseating smell around him, not to be seen again that night.

He had managed to garner from his client that, inexplicably, she liked him and would see him again. Things went slightly better that time. Ashley pulled out the stops. He found out more about her, what she liked and where was good to go. Reservations were made, and the dinner progressed without him screwing it up. The evening had laughter, great food, conversation and flirtatious touches of arms both ways. All was good. A few more dates later and they ended up in bed. It was the most intense and passionate experience Ashley had ever had.

When it came for him to return to the UK six months into their relationship, he didn't just ask her to come with him, he asked her to marry him. They got hitched high above the hills in Rio with the backdrop of Christ the Redeemer and the city below.

Since those heady days, they had two boys, Charlie and Harry, but the incessant grey skies in the UK had somewhat dampened her joie de vivre and sense of abandon Or was that just getting older as happens to everyone? Even so, whenever they met people, the usual reaction was 'wow, he's sure punching above his weight.'

She drove him to the newly acquired rugby club which was forty minutes west of London. He was still waiting to get his licence back after coming to the end of a six-month ban for being over the limit. He'd been out to lunch with a client only to be told by his dining companion that his services were no longer needed. Seeing as he was paying, Ashley decided to have the last drop of wine left in the bottle rather than pour it for the guy who'd just given him the Spanish Archer (*El Bow*). The ex-client had consumed most of the bottle, and there wasn't even a half glass left. When he pulled out in front of a police car while trying to put the seatbelt on, Havers was nabbed. The resultant breath test indicated being a fraction over. Blood alcohol levels have no leeway, so a tiny fraction over is still over and thus a criminal offence. Thais picked him up from the cop station and made his life hell for a few weeks. For the first one, she never said a word, simply stared at him in disgust, sucked in air through her teeth and shook her head. It was only when they worked through the practicalities of what it meant to their lives that things got heated. The endless ferrying to play dates, sports matches, sleepovers and extracurricular activities (always on a Saturday) gave her anger a renewed vigour. Her schedules of spas, shopping and socialising were seriously affected, something she resented Ashley for and all because he had no self-control with that glass of wine.

Before getting to the club, they drove up the so-called High Street. The first thing to strike them was how there could be so many people in the area who ate fried chicken. Apart from a different sign, what could one shop possibly offer that's different to the establishment next door? Perhaps less cat as an ingredient or a proud boast that only a few cockroaches had been found in their kitchens. Although the abundance of terrible takeaways was an indicator of the area's vibe, nothing gave it away more than the people out and about. People were walking big dogs on ropes mixed with other rabid-looking dogs without ropes or any owners for that matter. The guys wore imitation branded trackies, trainers and hoodies. Most were smoking reefers and seemed to sense the presence of a stranger. The girls had a particular penchant for cheap knockoff Uggs not suited for the rain. As they drove past, the Wayne and Waynettas turned their scrawny, pale heads in their hoodies and stared like angry zombies. Thank heavens for the sat nav, if Ashley had to ask directions of any of this lot, they'd eat their flesh. Thais looked scared.

The club was in a part of the Badcock area that was the rough end of a trading estate, if such a thing existed. It wasn't a nice bit of town but considering the bar wasn't high in the first place, it was a bad indictment.

"In one hundred yards, turn left into Pikey Lane," the sat nav instructed. Ashley thought it had to be wrong, the turning into the lane had a burned-out car on the corner. The scorched empty frame looked like a relatively recent development. He expanded the map, and moved it around left and right just to confirm that Badcock RFC was indeed at the end of that lane with no other way in. It was the most pleasant bit so far, just a plain, tree-lined lane. They came to a halt at the entrance to the club's grounds after five minutes. It was an old metal gate that had been reduced to just two posts. At the foot of one of them was a green wooden sign saying 'Welcome to Badcock Town RFC' in white letters. Some joker had used white paint to make the 'c' a capital and had added an 's' at the end to make 'BadCocks'.

On entering the car park, they pulled up to where a few vehicles were parked. Sandwiched in between them was a very old motorhome with the front wheels replaced with bricks. Ashley was gathering his stuff from the front of the car when the door motorhome door flew open to reveal Shane Walton, a fat man with tattoos, a mullet, in his boxer shorts and vest. He let a large wolf-looking thing out that promptly defecated on the tarmac in between him and Ashley's car. Shane just stared at Ashley, so too did the dog whilst doing his business. Then when the creature went back in, Shane scratched his undercarriage, broke wind and followed, shutting the door behind him.

4

The clubhouse entrance was a double-panelled glass door with one side almost completely shattered and held together with masking tape. Through the doors followed a cold, damp, long corridor that smelt of deep heat. A notice board was halfway down with various bits of paper badly stuck to it. A sign showed the lounge bar was to the left. Ashley burst in with gusto. The floor was a brown swirly carpet that a grandma from the 19th century would have been proud of. It looked as though it'd been there since the 50s. The stickiness underfoot came from the accumulation of all the drinks spilt on it over the years. An assortment of different-sized tables and chairs made up the seating area. Various pictures of Jockey and other players festooned the walls. A bar stretched the width of the room at the back with all the six nations' flags pinned up above. Howley sat at the bar, pint of Guinness on the go, wearing the ubiquitous Wales top. Behind, wiping glasses, was Breeda, with voluminous flame-red hair overflowing in tempestuous curls. His entrance got the merest of acknowledgement from the occupants. Howley picked up his pint and took a sip before addressing the new owner.

"Can I help boyo?" he asked in a gravelly, Richard Burton voice.

"I'm looking for Howley Davies."

"Well you found him." Ashley moved forward to shake his hand.

"I'm Ashley Havers." Howley took another gulp of his pint, put it down, stood up and shook.

"Are you now? What will you have to drink?" Breeda shot Ashley a stare verging on the angry.

"Have you got Camomile tea?"

"Ah sure we have. We also have rose water peppermint and herbal tea." Breeda said in a thick Dublin accent.

"Camomile would be great, thanks." Breeda stared in disbelief.

"She's joking. This is a rugby club bar, we're not big on the Camomile here. We could rustle up a fine cup of builders' for you."

"Oh, ok, just water's fine."

"Rose petal or rosemary?" Breeda asked as the two men sat down at a table. Ashley didn't want to take this further so smiled and nodded with a mental note to sort out the sarcastic one.

They exchanged pleasantries about Jockey, Breeda slapped down a glass of water looking like it came from the drains and smirked.

"You know he gave me this club in his will?"

"Of course, put a lot of noses out of joint."

"How come?"

"There are folk who've been here long enough to remember leather balls." In the old days, a rugby ball was leather. Considering the game is played in the rain and mud, this was not an ideal combination. It became like a bar of soap and as heavy as a brick. The modern-day rubber/polyester ball, whilst still getting slippery when wet, was nothing like these old incarnations. This reference was completely lost on Ashley. "They were close to Jockey, they wanted to take over the legacy from him. They think it was their rite," Howley continued.

"You've been here a long time right?"

"Don't worry. I couldn't give a shit about my legacy or what I'm owed. I'm just here coaching until I'm given the boot or can no longer stand." He took out a cigarette and lit it. Ashley was shocked and stared at the Welshman in horror. Howley came from a time when everyone smoked in pubs, nightclubs, planes, tube trains and even hospitals. Yes, the law made it illegal to light up inside any public places but who was going to tell on him?

"Erm, what are you doing?" Howley took a drag, fixed him with a tired stare and raised his eyebrows to say 'You're in my domain now.' "I would rather you didn't, it's disgusting." Howley sighed, took another drag and put the cigarette out. He made sure the smoke was blown into Ashley's space making him cough and waft.

"It's not me that's upset, others."

"I don't know if you've gathered, but I really am at a bit of a loss as to why I'm here."

"Old Jocks had a good sense of humour."

"What am I supposed to do?"

"You could always get your boots on for a run out with the vets." The coach might as well have been talking to himself.

"So Howley, what's this rugby all about then?" Howley heaved another big sigh and looked up to the sky.

"Jockey you king Charlie." He turned back to Havers. "It can be boiled down to this: two lots of players going at each other for eighty minutes trying to score more points than the other lot,"

"How do they do that?"

"Tries and goals."

"Ah like football," Ashley thought he had done OK with his bluff.

"Look, get this joke, then you'll get rugby," Howley said.

"OK, fire away."

"What do you call a bunch of guys hanging around with rugby players?"

"I don't know, what do you call a bunch of guys hanging around with rugby players?"

"Backs." Of course Ashley didn't get it and there was an awkward silence. "I suppose I'd better show you around then."

"That would be great, I just need to do an important email, what's the wi-fi network called?" Ashley asked holding up his phone.

"The cocks," Breeda snorted.

"Oh."

"A joke from Sheriff Woody who installed it," she continued.

"I've not heard of that network before."

"He's the handyman and a complete cowboy. He also did the

leccie, so be careful plugging anything in."

The tour started in the kitchen off the right-hand side of the bar. Like the lounge, it too had seen better days and wouldn't have survived a health inspection by the council. Whoever handled stocking up on food and cooking utensils, had clearly been dead for many years.

"You cook food in here?" Ashley asked.

"The bacon rolls are the best in the county."

"That's it?"

"We can do a pot noodle or heat something up in the microwave. It's all we've ever needed."

They moved into the corridor and stopped in front of the notice board. There were various flyers for pizza and burger takeaways. One advertised a social event at the club from three years ago. The Badcock RFC 1st XV v Nobbler's Wold 1st XV team sheet was two years old.

"Not much call for notices then?" Ashley pointed out.

"All done in the WhatsApp group now."

The tour then took in the changing rooms, kit room, what was laughingly called the gym and the committee room. It didn't take long.

When Ashley exited the clubhouse, Shane was smoking again with the dog roaming. Slightly scared, he hurried past mullet man and got in the car. They watched as he picked up a washing line, attached it to either end of the motorhome and started hanging stuff up from a laundry bag. He looked over at Ashley and Thais, nodded and then started removing extreme S&M items. A gimp suit, various studded leather underpants, a horse's tail attached to something shiny that neither of them knew was, a harness and furry handcuffs. With each item that came out, Ashley and Thais' jaws dropped a few more inches. Shane finished, looked at the collection, nodded in appreciation and disappeared back into the motorhome.

"Man has dog it poo everywhere," Thais remarked. They both sniffed and looked down to discover he'd stepped in one of the mutt's deposits.

"Oh God!" Ashley shrieked. He jumped out and started scraping his shoe along the ground leaving the car door open.

"Hans invite us Mykonos half term," Thais said after they reached the relative safety of the motorway back into London and the smell had gone. "I say yes."

"I hate Mykonos not least because you need a new mortgage for lunch and people there are so far up their own arses, they brush their teeth through their navels"

"You hate all my friends."

"Not your Brazilian ones, just the super-entitled ones, which is most of them these days." In fact, most of Thais' friends were funny, always loved a laugh and he liked them. There were as rich as Croesus but that wasn't his issue. No, his issue was Hans. He never hated anyone in his life, apart from this guy. Thais had met him, pre-Ashley, back in Rio when he was doing business there. They dated for a few months before Hans went back. Ashley still didn't understand what business he did but talking about it always involved dropping names like bombs, talking telephone number deals and about how brilliant he was. Ashley referred to him as 'OCC' i.e., overconfident cock, something he soon learned not to say around Thais. This moniker came about when he met Hans at a wedding. He truly lived up to the nickname, in particular heckling the groom's speech with completely unfunny interjections about cocks and private jets. He never asked a single question to Ashley and regarded him as something akin to Shane dog's deposit. So for this reason, Ashley hated Mykonos. That was Hans' playground. He lorded it up, boasted, showed off his connections, money and of course - himself. If you took that guy out of the equation, Ashley would actually enjoy going to the beautiful Greek island, even if the prices made him weep.

"I can't go, I've got this place. It will be the end of the season, important time. I don't get the club until the end of the season. We could be bust, we could be ok, who knows?"

"When get over Hans thing?"

"You go, take the kids, I really need to be here." Inside, he breathed a huge sigh of relief.

"You take pervert Shrek over Mykonos?"

5

The venue for Ashley's first committee meeting was the deeply shabby club boardroom. The wooden filing cabinet in the corner looked as though it had been Noah's on the Ark. It was held together by string and gaffer tape as were most of the chairs. The wallpaper's style matched the swirly carpet downstairs in the bar. David sat at the table wearing the same blazer and tie he wore at the ashes spreading. Ashley was in the usual chinos and polo top. Thais had tried many times to stop him from looking like something out of a Bowden catalogue and get a bit of style into his wardrobe. Every bit of clothing she ever bought for him, made his skin itch. He just wasn't comfortable being trendy or stylish and always reverted to the uniform of type. There was a little wooden sign in front of David that said *Club Secretary*. Next to him was Ritchie Sanders, in his 60s, wearing a horrific incarnation of the 'I'm fun, honestly' Hawaiian shirt. He was very thin on top but the sides of his dyed blonde hair protruded out at right angles. His little nameplate said *Social Secretary*. Ashley looked at him and Howley and thought they must go to the same hairdresser, one that looked after men of a certain age who didn't want to look anything like that age. The table creaked as David put his elbows on it and ruffled some papers. One of the pictures fell off the wall just beside Ashley making him jump and yelp. David, Howley and Ritchie, unmoved, just left it.

"So how's the club financially?" Ashley asked.

"We're so poor, we can't even pay attention," David informed him.

"Oh."

"And we'll be going bust at the end of this season."

"But didn't Jockey put a lot of money in?" Ashley asked.

"Freddie The Fix, stole it all," Howley piped in.

"Who's that?"

"The accountant."

"Well there's got to be something we can do, make savings somewhere or do something to earn money," Ashley chimed.

"You're the rich one Ashley. Jockey left the club to you. Surely you've got that to chuck in the pot?" David said.

"Ah, I'm a bit strapped at the moment. In between jobs with an expensive family and a ball-crushing mortgage. So no, surprisingly, I don't have a hundred k."

"We should have a rave man!" Ritchie said. Howley and David laughed out loud.

"Well that's an idea isn't it?" Ashley asked.

"He's 62, the last rave he went to, Pat Sharpe was the DJ," spat Howley.

"Man, we have the space, the licence and the lads," Ritchie pleaded.

"Well it's worth a go no?" asked Ashley.

"It's not going to solve a thing. 100k, that's what we need to survive," David spat. "You need to come up with something or else it's the knacker's yard for us," he assured. They all sat looking at Ashley in silence.

"He's pissed off because he was hoping he'd get the club, he'd been here longer than Stonehenge," said Howley.

"I'll thank you to leave talk like that out Howley. I am a servant of the club, it's in my blood and bones. And I will work in the best interests of the club to ensure its survival. A rave isn't."

"One thing I've learned is that in an open forum, barriers are erected when the word 'no' comes into the discussion. There's no such thing as a bad idea," Havers offered up.

"You just said it," Howley jumped in.

"What?"

"You just brought up 'no' telling us we can't use 'no'." Ashley looked confused but carried on.

"Anyway, if someone suggests an idea, it's never a bad one."

"It is when Ritchie has it," Howley snorted.

"Well Ritchie, I like it. It's a start and who knows what could happen. You're in charge do your stuff." David and Howley sighed in unison.

His next trip to the club, Ashley drove himself. He'd finally gotten his licence back, which was a blessing for all concerned. Thais no longer had to ferry him and the kids around. Ashley could do his fair share of school runs, playdates and the rest of it. She made him do more than that out of punishment for putting them in that position in the first place. So when he wasn't at the club, he was driving offspring somewhere.

"Glad I found you Ritchie, I wanted to talk to you about the rave ad," he said on finding the Social Director in the clubhouse corridor.

"The posters have gone all over the town, then there's the socials and everything. Ballistic man," Ritchie said. He was proud as Punch with his efforts. Ashley called it up on his phone from the group chat that he'd been added to by Howley.

"You don't think it's er..." Ashley said.

"Brilliant?"

"Not quite the word I had in mind."

"Why what's wrong?"

"First off, why a smurf?"

"The club once had a nickname of the smurfs."

"I'm afraid to ask but why?"

"There was once a hooker in the firsts, Jimbo Smurf, who had a particular trick in the scrum. He specialised in reaching down and across in front of him." Ritchie did the action with his arm and hand reaching out, palm open like he'd just bowled a strike. "And squeezing the knackers of the opposing hooker until he was blue in the face." He squeezed as though he was really doing it. "All without ever getting the refs attention. Although they would always wonder why the scrum would break up for no reason from his view with both front rows swinging at each other." Ritchie smirked as he remembered those times.

"I now know the smurf reference, thanks Ritchie. What are all those white drops coming out the top of his head?"

"That's the sweat coming out because Jimbo's got his baby makers in his grip."

"OK. And you don't think the positioning of the two rugby balls on the ground under said smurf cause any problems with you?"

"What do you mean?"

"Follow me." He led him into the bar where Breeda was leaning against the bar swiping photos on an iPad, shaking her head in disgust at each photo. She looked up when they came in.

"Are you responsible for this filth, yer little gobshite yer," she spat at Ritchie.

"What's wrong," he asked.

"Because a huge eegit advertised a rave here at the club, all over town, using a blue cock and balls, all the filthy feckers have sent in their own versions on our socials. Disgusting." She looked down and swiped again. "Ah jaysus, that's just a twiglet and two cashew nuts."

"Sorry Ritchie, I have a meeting now," Ashley said, "But I reckon you might want to take those posters down, don't you?" Ritchie left disgruntled but nonetheless, slightly embarrassed.

Havers sat down and opened his laptop. He was meeting Fortesque Smythe. Despite not having a clue who this grand sounding gent was, the new owner took advice from Sarah, who brokered the powwow, but it needed to be at the club.

"This isn't connecting to the wifi," Ashley said annoyed.

"It's fecked today and Woody's on holiday," Breeda helpfully informed him. Howley and 'Budgie' sat at the back of the bar beside the toilet door, as they read newspapers. Budgie was a second row in the firsts. A man-mountain who stood 6ft6in with a face that had been trodden on more times than hot dinners and ears that any caterpillar would happily chomp on if they were green. He had played for England B's a few times, but simply wasn't good enough to break into the senior side. His claim to fame from those days was breaking the nose of another second row who then went on to be a brilliant captain for England. The two players shared a few beers after the match, the injured one having a load of tissue shoved up his fattened and swollen nose. Budgie was proper old school and believed in the ethos, spirit and the values most players and the game itself hold true. His real name was Courtney Beaumont but Budgie was his name at BRFC. Long before the world ever heard about a famous South African's caks, Courtney always wore a pair of budgie smugglers in a match, from his first ever proper club game. The big fella got up, tucked the newspaper under his arm and headed into the gents.

"One in the chamber," he said proudly.

"Open a damn window," barked Howley.

Fortesque walked through the squeaky doors into the bar. His physique rivalled Julian's, even his hands looked as though they needed a diet. His fingers were like chipolatas, as if ran into a wall leading with them. He wore a green tweed jacket, a country check shirt and red jeans. He looked every inch the landowner he was. Everyone else in there ignored him, they'd met him before. Ashley stood up and offered his hand. In a place like BTRFC's clubhouse, when someone like that walks in, Havers made no mistake this was his 3 O'clock.

"Ashley, pleased to meet you." Fortesque gave him the wet fish, a handshake that wouldn't break the skin on custard, and glanced off somewhere in the distance. This immediately irritated Ashley. No matter what background you came from, a firm (not too firm) handshake and eye contact were a prerequisite of gentlemanly behaviour. "Can I offer you a drink?"

"Breeda knows what I'll have."

"Oh, OK, well the usual for me please Breeda." After some faffing about pulling out notebooks whose only purpose was to show that people are taking notes in a very important meeting, she brought over a couple of pints of bitter in jug glasses.

"Ah Breeda, you know I'm on the tea," Ashley proffered.

"You're gonna need this, believe me," she said and slammed both pints on the table spilling a fair bit. As she bent down,

Smythe letched down her top. She caught him, stood up, picked up his pint and threw most of it over him.

"Oops, sorry about that. Are you ok?" Breeda said sarcastically. Fortesque was about to fly into a rage, but he looked at Breeda giving him evils and held back.

"Where can I plug this in?" Fortesque said holding up a phone charger. Breeda nodded at a socket bedside him. Her and Ashley watched intensely as he plugged in the phone. They moved their heads away as if expecting something to blow.

"Nice to meet a fellow owner," Ashley said.

"You're not a real owner. The Spartans has been in my family for generations."

"Like the clap!" muttered Breeda loudly back behind the bar, seething. The Spartans were the county's best side. They had a wonderful ground with modern facilities everywhere. Although its top teams played in a couple of leagues, and were thus semi-professional, they also had an amateur team for up-and-coming stars used as a feeder into the better teams. Although registering Breeda's comment, Fortesque continued, "It's part of our land in the county for generations."

"Folks, meet the wife oh, she's also my sister." Breeda couldn't help herself. Ashley shot a disapproving look her way which was dismissed with the Irish death stare, something no one should be on the end of.

"In fact we'll own this land as soon as there is no longer a functioning rugby club on it," Fortesque continued.

"That's the first I've heard of it." Budgie came back out of the toilet and sat down.

"Yes, it's a clause in the title that goes back to my great grand pa-paa. The title of the land was granted to the rugby club in the 1800s. This runs out at the end of this season and reverts back to our family if there is no longer a functioning rugby club on it."

"Now I know what Jockey wanted me to do, stop you doing that." Ashley stated. Fortesque got up in a strop. He unplugged the charger and got a small electric shock, something that amused everyone apart from him. He headed to the toilet door.

"I assume it's safe to use the toilet in this awful place?" he asked as he passed.

"Well I'd give it a few..." the landowner didn't hear Howley's warning and barged through the door only to re-emerge after a couple of seconds holding his nose and gagging.

"Dear god! Someone's died in there."

6

Josh came into the club bar, Breeda half acknowledged him. He was visiting from Singapore and was keen to see the club his old mate had been landed with. He'd just about finished laughing since he first heard about a man who knew nothing about rugby, inheriting a rugby club.

"I noticed a motorhome in the carpark on bricks, is my car safe here?" Josh asked.

"It's not that bad, just don't leave it here overnight."

"There also seemed to be the odd picture of a blue dick around on my way in?"

"Stupid fecker," Breeda hissed. Josh got a pint, Ash on the tea, and they sat down in the corner.

"I bet Thais loves your new career direction. This is bang up her street," Josh said sarcastically. Ashley was not ugly but also hardly Brad Pitt. He was just very middle-of-the-road, nice and normal. Havers thought that to really impress someone like Thais, he needed to over-egg his wealth to stand a chance with her. He didn't lie, just didn't go out of his way to correct assumptions that were made about how much money he had. When they met at that party in Rio, he'd built up a successful PR agency with offices in London, Manchester and six foreign locations. It was possibly worth quite a sum, but it hadn't made him enough money to fly on private jets. Its profit margins were tiny as the work was so labour-intensive and the fees only really covered the costs each year. But it looked good to outside eyes, and when Tais googled him after the evening, it looked impressive. The group collapsed in financial turmoil and skulduggery a few years after returning to the UK. He didn't make any money out of the hard work he'd put into building up the company.

"We're going to sell it as soon as we can," Ashley whispered so as not to let Breeda hear. "The problem is that a condition of Jockey's will means I can't sell it until the end of the season and the club needs to be in the black."

"Easy enough right?"

"It's totally broke and about to go bankrupt. If that happens, I lose the right to the land, which could mean missing out on a fortune, money we really need. I don't know how we can possibly make the money."

"Is the team any good?" Josh asked. He knew the answer to that but wanted to see what Ashley would say.

"I have no idea myself but according to everyone, including the coach, they're absolutely shocking."

"Ah, well I was going to suggest The Hunt Sewage Tournament." Josh had googled the club when he found out about his friend being the new owner. He discovered an annual county tournament, unsurprisingly sponsored by Hunt Sewage. It took its name from a family who owned sewage processing sites across the county. The tournament was affectionately known locally as 'the shit' tournament, although not when any Hunt family members were in earshot. It was open to all non-professional teams in the county. There were five preliminary rounds, all structured in a knockout format. These opening fixtures were all drawn out of a hat, there was no seeding so the two top teams could meet in round one with a possible favourite not making it through. This flew in the face of most tournament planning; it was never good to lose a fancied team in the first round. Most competitions make sure the minnows or no-hopers are paired up with top teams in the first stages, so the excitement builds throughout the tourney. But the Hunt family thought it made for more jeopardy, more excitement and the chance of shocks, which they saw as more fun. After the prelims, there was the semi and a final. The venue for the final would again be drawn from a hat, the hat consisting of the two finalists. The prize for the winner was £100k.

"We could go for that," Ashley stated after hearing the details.

"A rugby club owned by a guy who knows nothing about rugby, coached by someone who, even he thinks his team are shit, a terrible ground and no experience in any sort of competitive competition. What could go wrong?"

"Why don't you join me, help me with it? You're Yoda when it comes to the game."

"I'll help you where I can, but I'm needed back in Singapore. I really wish you the best of luck, man you're going to need it."

It was committee meeting time again.

"I want to talk to you about the Hunt Sewage Tournament," Ashley proclaimed.

"Don't worry about it," Howley sniffed.

"If we won it, there's a hundred k prize."

"I'm guessing you know dim byd about rugby and you've certainly never seen us play."

"It's a cup, and even I know about those, everyone has a chance don't they?"

"This lot wouldn't win if they were the only team playing," David chimed in. Howley nodded in agreement.

"You said I need to get a 100k and so here is a good opportunity to do that – with a bit of change on top."

"There's more chance of Budgie beating Usain Bolt than these guys getting past the first round," Howley said.

"We're entered into the tournament, and we're going to win it you know. I feel it in my bones." Howley and David laugh hysterically.

"The All Blacks are shitting themselves," Howley said.

"I don't think you should bring race into it Howley." said Ashley.

"Not exactly the best plan to get the money, I hope you've got a better one than that," said the Secretary.

"I have plenty of plans, don't you worry about that."

"Let's hear them then," David challenged.

"They're under formulation and being blue-skied as we

speak," Ashley lied.

"Being what?" Howley asked.

"Discussed in an open forum is what that means."

"More like pie in the blue sky," Howley taunted.

"They're not being discussed here," David pointed out.

"They will be, they will be, I can assure you. Anyway, how are plans for tonight's rave going?" Ritchie suddenly woke up as if he'd been poked with a sharp stick.

"All good, going to be a stonker man!" Ritchie exclaimed.

"Ha ha, like having a shite at a funeral home more like," they heard Breeda's voice coming from somewhere. It was like she was listening at the door. They all looked around as if something supernatural had happened. Ashley got up to look out of the window and saw Shane smoking, drinking out of a can of Tennents Super whilst giving whistling at the wandering wolf.

"Who is that guy?" Ashley asked.

"Who?"

"There's only one guy in the car park at the moment with a tinnie, a fag, a bison for a pet and his home on bricks."

"Tarface," David stated.

"Why's he called that?"

"He used to work on the roads. Then one day, he managed to get tar on his knob that permanently stained it. How he managed that is a mystery, but it's fair to say, he's a sausage short of a barbie," Howley said.

"I still don't get it."

"He moved from the roads into crime and gangsters."

"How did he get here?"

"Not sure. About ten years ago, he just appeared with that motorhome."

"And he's still in the carpark of my rugby club?"

"No one's told him to leave."

"I will. It's not good luck for us to have something akin to the missing link and its canine, occupying the car park."

"Someone please film that, please," Howley implored.

7

Ashley found Howley standing beside the team bus in the carpark. It would have been modern – in the 60s. The rave of the century, as Ritchie called it, was only an hour away. Shane had scrubbed up, as far as he could, with an 80s shiny shellsuit that any football hooligan from that era would have been proud of. His box-fresh, expensive brand, white trainers, screamed knock-off. Howley pulled up the side luggage compartment of the bus that nearly fell off its hinges. It was stacked with cans and barrels of beer.

"Now give us a hand," he said to Ashley.

"Is that the best use of the team bus?"

"It's the only use," Howley said as he lifted a crate of beer out. Ashley picked up the smallest and lightest pack of cans. Howley sighed and shook his head.

"It's an old croquet injury. Really bad for my back," Ashley explained. Budgie arrived and hauled out a barrel as though it were a feather.

"Glad you're here," Ashley stated.

"I'm the security."

"Ah good, no undesirables will get past you eh." Budgie looked at him and shrugged. "Doing it with Tarface."

Badcock Town RFC's night didn't exactly hit he heights of its billing. Not much effort had been made to dress the place in its party clothes. The main lights had been turned down and a dancefloor area had been cleared in front of Ritchie who was in the corner doing his DJ thing. A small number of coloured lights flashed randomly from his so-called booth, which was basically a crate with a silver blanket over it. His fit-inducing Hawaiian shirt was bright yellow, bright pink, green and all manner of other colour combinations. He did the prescribed DJ actions. From Fatboy Slim to the worst wedding DJ ever, they all had a number of actions that defined their set. The bog-standard staple was to put the headphones on, then lift off one side, fiddle with some buttons, look up, perhaps raise one hand, and nod. The nod was very important, it was an indication of how good their music was, even when it wasn't. A sip of a drink whilst still in the rhythm, then back to the full headphones, a bit of dancing, more single-use headphone, etc. Repeat all night, especially if there's no one dancing, which there wasn't. The turnout had been sparse from the beginning. Most players had left with their partners at about 9 pm, claiming babysitter trouble. It seemed that babysitters had been thin on the ground this one night in Badcock. Nevertheless, those guys had shown their support, shown their faces then shown their backs as they ran for the horror that was the party.

By 10 pm it was even worse. There were six players left. Breeda was just looking at her phone behind the bar, occasionally she looked over to Ritchie when he put on another terrible song and shouted

"'For fuck's sake Ritchie, it's 2022 not 1922." There were a few guys that were 'friends' of Tarface, taking up a corner of the bar, wearing a lot of fake gold and scowling at anyone who looked in their general direction. The muscle on the door had long given up the lost cause as no-one at all was coming in.

"I don't think this makes a viable money-making opportunity going forward, do you?" David asked Ashley after sitting down.

"God, it's awful. He's like someone the care home brought in to do the entertainment at lunchtime."

"You didn't listen when I told you." Out of the window a blue flashing light could be seen reflecting on all the surfaces. Two police officers walked in, looked around and moved towards the gang in the corner. When police enter a party, it has an immediate effect, making people stop and stare. Howley got up from his stool at the bar and greeted them, there was a bit of conversation, then he stepped aside letting the officers approach the swarthy-looking gang.

"What do they want?" Ash asked as Howley re-joined them.

"They are investigating that lot dealing drugs," he said as he pointed at Mr motorhome's associates.

"Shane has to go, I'm not putting up with this stuff."

Howley just shrugged and said, "It's all right, I know the coppers, we play rugby against them. I'll make it go away."

"And also, for the record, we're not letting that man DJ ever again." Ashley said to the departing Howley.

Ashley got back home a little worse for wear, he'd had more than he should have or normally had. He needed it to numb the awfulness of the club and the rave. As he came through the door of their Victorian terraced house in the expensive area of Notting Hill, he heard Thais laughing in the sitting room. There he discovered the blood boiler (Hans) drinking champagne with his wife on the sofa. She got up, kissed him, Hans shook his hand and said he needed the loo.

"What's Euro von dickhead doing here?"

"You drunk?"

"I had a couple of beers," he said, falling dramatically into one of the armchairs.

"You no drink."

"It was our rave at the club. Right on man!" he said making a half-hearted v sign. "Anyway, you haven't answered my question."

"He got buyers for club."

"Has he now? Do they know anything about rugby?"

"You know nothing about rugby."

"I'm learning."

"Stop being that. Bed for you." Hans came back in clutching his phone.

"I've got to go, closing meeting on a billion-dollar deal tomorrow morning. Chao." Thais got up.

"I'll show you out." Hans didn't say anything to Ashley as they walked out.

"Bye Hans," he mumbled to himself. When she came back in, Ashley had slumped to almost falling out of the chair onto the floor. His eyes were putting up a last stand.

"He sounds like an Abba tribute act," Ashley muttered to himself.

"Get over we date before. We just friends," she spat as Ashley's eyes closed and he checked out. She turned the lights out as she left.

He was in the doghouse for a few days and had more errands to run than usual. With the school run done, he decided to try out the gym at the club. That noun was stretching it beyond all credulity. It wasn't even a weights room, more a large, cold cupboard with a couple of benches and a few weights resting on the floor. It was the sort of place equipment at his swanky (and expensive) London gym went to die unceremoniously. If he thought the weights room was cold, then the changing rooms took it up a notch, or down many notches if measured on a thermometer. The walls were originally green but there was very little evidence of that left, with all the exposed brickwork and flaking paint. It had a similar look to some gastropub in a trendy up-and-coming area. That phrase usually meant just plain awful but it was just a way for the people who lived there, to big it up. It was damp and smelled of mud. A few discarded socks, a gumshield, a pair of shorts and some strapping mixed in the mud under the long benches. He dumped his bag on one of them and undressed quickly. He congratulated himself on bringing the crocs. Thais hated them and said he looked like an out-of-work dentist, but he lived them, and now they were paying for themselves, making sure his bare feet never touched the floor. He grabbed his towel and headed off to the showers. There were prison facilities with more welcoming sights. 6 pipes came out of the wall, only two had shower heads, and two were just dripping like sad plumbers' mistakes. He chose the one at the end and looked for somewhere to put his towel, there was nowhere other than a half wall marking the shower area. When he turned the tap on, what came out over him was brown water that must have been taken from a leaking freezer. The chill cut through to the bone. He would have shrieked if his voice had not temporarily deserted him in shock. He immediately turned it off. Shivering, he grabbed his towel and headed back to the changing room. Greeting him in there when he entered was Faf du Preez staring at him and chewing gum vigorously like he had something against it. The unexpected visitor made him almost shriek again for the second time in the space of a few seconds. Faf was the firsts' captain and scrum-half. He was bald but had clearly been a gym monkey for many a year. He rippled and bulged in a too-tight t-shirt, even his little ears had muscles. He wasn't going to challenge anyone in height competition unless they were aged 14, but his legs were so thick, he couldn't close them together.

"Yo bro," he managed to say without breaking chewing.

"Christ, you scared the shit out of me."

"I'm Faf."

"I'm Ashley."

"Ya I know bro."

"I would shake your hand but I'm holding a towel up."

"Don't mind me." Ashley turned, still shivering, dried himself and started dressing.

"What the hell is going on with those showers?" Ashley asked.

"Hot water went years ago."

"They should bring heart attack victims here, that'll revive them."

"I s'pose."

"Why has no-one called a plumber to fix them?" Faf just shrugged. "So what's your story here?"

"I was a bok bro, now I'm the best player here."

"A what?"

"Best player."

"No, what was that other word you said?"

"A bok, a Springbok."

"You were an animal?"

"Jesus bro, a rugby player for South Africa -the country right."

"Ah, I see, what position do you play?" Ashley asked still not knowing the ins and outs of rugby positions.

"Second row," Faf said dismissively.

"Oh righty ho."

"That's a joke. I'm scrum-half bro, Jesus."

"I'm still getting to grips with all the rugby slang."

"So we're playing the sewage tournament?"

"Yep, could be great for the club."

"Funny really," Faf smirked.

"Oh yes, why's that?"

"We've been shit for years."

"Oh well that's going to change."

"How do you plan on doing that bro?" Ashley had finished dressing now, still shivering though.

"Have you heard of TCUP?" Ashley asked. Faf looked at him as though he was going mad. "Thinking Clearly Under Pressure. When you guys are under pressure in a game, you need to make the right decisions to win." Josh had given him a link to one of Sir Clive Woodward's management mantras.

"The only pressure we have is getting to the bog before Budgie."

"I've seen that in action. Anyway, I've got a surprise for you guys today before training." Ashley said.

"Ohh can't wait bro. So what's your job?"

"I'm in PR, I run a successful consultancy helping brands get their name out there."

"PR you say," Faf said laughing. "Did you ever tackle a 120 kilo winger running at full pelt?"

"I had to deal with a very nasty Prime Minister's press secretary once, that's scary."

"Yah bru, sounds terrifying eh." As Ashley packed his gym bag, Faf raised his arms, flexed his biceps and admired them. Ashley's not looking at him. "So what do you press?"

"Oh I leave that to the cleaner," Ashley said as he left the changing room.

The committee room hadn't seen so much action in years. Ashley and Howley were in it, a whiteboard separated them. On the top page TCUP was written in big letters on the top.

"Jesus, PR!" Howley sighed. Faf had told them about their little tete-a-tete.

"Forget that Howley, you need to see what success looks like for us."

"I do, it's getting the players out of the pub on game day."

"We need to plan for the 1st plan, then the 2nd plan."

"Makes total sense."

"This is all about TCUP–thinking clearly under pressure," Ashley said pointing at the whiteboard.

"I'm thinking very clearly, that this is a pile of shite."

"I want you to come up with some training with plays to be done at certain pressure points of the game. When players know what to do in those situations, they won't panic and make the wrong choices."

"What do you think a coach does?"

"Not much by the look of it."

"Careful now boyo."

"Well, we've got a month until the first game, so you need to get a move on don't you." Howley shook his head, sighed and stood up.

"I don't like you or your bullshit but I will do it your way - for him." He said, pointing at a portrait of Jockey half hanging off the wall. He moved to the door. "And only for him."

"Excellent Howley, that's the spirit."

"Then when we go out in the first game, you can shove your TCUP somewhere very painful and dark."

8

Ashley and Howley watched on the sideline as the team trained, it was raining for a change.

"How are they doing?" Ashley asked. Howley just sighed and gestured to the pitch where the hooker, Brian Thompson, was throwing into the lineout. He aimed and then threw it so hard and crooked, it missed everyone and landed in the opposition half.

"He's called Shambles."

"Which one?"

"The one who just threw that lineout."

"Why's he called that?" Ashley was expecting some funny story about how a player got his nickname, but Howley just looked at him in disgust.

"Because he's a shambles." Another training play and the ball came out of the scrum. Faf threw a pass to the fly-half, Owen Wilkinson, handsome, big hair and buff. He waited for the ball, but it went over his head and went to ground. Faf had a go at Wilkinson, blaming him. Howley shook his head.

"Van Der Westhuzian he is not."

"I don't know if that's good or not. I do know that pass was bad. He told me he's our best player."

"He thinks he is."

"Said he was a Bok." Ashley said proud that he could repeat a rugby term without prompting.

"He trialled for them when a kid. The nearest he got to the full side was carrying their kit."

"At least he's got to be strong with all that muscle right?"

"Might as well be jelly, it's the roids."

"The what?"

"Bodybuilding steroids. Also turns them mad as a box of frogs." A tattooed man in his fifties with a shaven head approached the pair.

"You the new owner then?" he asked Ashley.

"Yes, pleased to meet you."

"My son's the best player here you know. Could be playing for England soon."

"Not this again Steve," Howley told him. The man moved off whilst shouting at the pitch.

"Who's his son?" asked Ashley. Howley pointed at the fullback, Dusty Robinson, as a high kick went up.

"Keep your eyes on it son," shouted Steve. The player set himself correctly for the ball, the breadbasket created, eyes on the ball and ready to turn as he caught it thus avoiding knocking on. Textbook stuff. The ball landed six feet to his right with the player rooted to the spot. He'd completely misjudged the flight of the ball.

"That's not a regulation ball," shouted Steve. Every club has a delusional dad, unable to see the truth that their offspring really aren't that good.

"Surely we've got some good players?" Ashley asked.

"The flanker's a proper unit and a good at jackalling, the wing's good off either foot and the fly-half punts well," Howley offered. Ashley had absolutely no idea what he was talking about but thought it best to bluff it out.

"Excellent Howley."

"Still playing pool with rope though."

"There's only a couple of weeks to go to the first match, I'm sure you can do it. I've got a little something up my sleeve for you and the team"

"I'll try to contain myself."

The 1sts were changing after training. Ashley walked in with Fiona Bullen who simply oozed fitness. In her early thirties, with cheekbones reserved for supermodels, her brunette hair was pulled back in a ponytail. She was in yoga leggings, sports top and trainers. Every visible sinew bristled like a coiled spring.

"Right chaps, I want to introduce you to the new director of physio and fitness - Fiona."

"Hi guys," she said confidently and waved. A few players were about to whistle but thought better of it. Tiny (6ft 6in second row whose real name was Martin Dooley) in just his jockstrap, stood up and raised one leg onto the bench.

"She's going to get you fit and look after your physical requirements," Ashley continued.

"I've got a physical requirement right here that needs attention," Tiny said gesticulating to his crotch. Some of the players laughed. Fiona walked up to him and grabbed his testicles, squeezing tightly. Tiny yelped and couldn't move.

"Two things," she whispered in his ear but loud enough for the others to still hear. Tiny squealed as she tightened her grip. "First, that's inappropriate behaviour that you'll never do again right?" The huge man shook his head. She squeezed tighter. "Second, it's up to me to choose what bits get attention, right?" he nodded painfully but silently. She released him and he collapsed onto the bench. "Let me educate you gentleman," she said having moved into the middle of the changing room. "I've been around naked men all my life." Even with such a setup, not one player moved a muscle or even smirked. "I've seen every type of meat and two veg out there. Your childish, sexist, play-acting doesn't faze me in the slightest. I have four brothers for God's sake." She was addressing a completely silent room. "I can tell you something though, you're going to work your arses off for me. I will torture you, make you puke, you will hate me but I will, by God, get you at least to some level of fitness."

Ashley stood outside the clubhouse with David as they watched her take the first training session. Various players had collapsed to their knees on the pitch, some were walking off as if they'd been in a war, two were throwing up. Faf and Owen were trying to outdo themselves to impress Fiona with overly aggressive training. They ran at each other, sledged and bumped chests in that 'oh yeah' sort of way. All handbags and she had none of it.

"Jesus, she's supposed to train them, not kill them," Ashley remarked.

"How on earth can we afford her? Have I not told you about our financial situation?" David said.

"She's doing it pro bono."

"What's U2 got to do with it?"

"It means she's doing it for free David." Unbeknown to everyone at the club, Fiona used to be called an it girl in the London noughties. She had famous friends, and they were always being papped at various events. She did charity work for causes such as mental health and dementia. But she wasn't just famous for being famous like so many social media stars. She had a successful fitness brand where she charged gold bullion levels of fees to train already pampered and spoiled celebs. The celeb endorsements drove the normal punters in their droves to her classes and threw money at her books. No one at Badcock would have ever heard of her, they were not of that crowd and had scant knowledge of London-centric goings on. An instructor at his gym put them in touch, and in one of those small world coincidences, she had history with Smythe. Her parents were divorced because he had an affair with her mother. She would have love nothing more than sticking it to 'that fat bastard' in her words.

They watched as budgie completed a sprint between two training cones. As he passed Fiona, he stopped with his hands on his thighs and panted like a dying wildebeest caught in a lion's death grip. She slapped him on the bottom.

"Well done lad," she shouted. Budgie smiled proudly and managed to straighten up, fill his lungs with air and jog off. Ashley moved down to the pitch and watched his kids run through some mini rugby moves with Howley and six other minis. They were all covered from head to toe in mud and absolutely loved every second of it. Thais had not wanted the children to play rugby at all, even the mini version, and definitely not anywhere like the full-contact, dangerous sport she was learning about. The senior players trooped off the pitch after their session. A couple looked as though they were crawling apart from Wilkinson who jogged around without a hair out of place. Fiona ran up and stopped beside Ashley.

"Where did you find those?" Ashley asked, spying the muddy rugby boots she wore.

"Shambles lent them to me, he said they were an old pair." Ashley didn't want to let on that they will have been out of the lost property box as that's where Shambles always got his boots. He didn't understand why players would fork out for a new pair when there were perfectly usable ones in that box.

"You might want to fumigate them next time." They watched the players go past.

"They need to play in a few weeks," Ashley said.

"What was their fitness training before?" Fiona asked.

"It mainly involved beer."

"You need to join us for a session."

"Thanks but I'm not suited to that sort of stuff," he lied. He had always tried to stay fit but just preferred the facilities and feel of his own club but didn't want to seem snobby to Fiona, and certainly didn't want to experience the Badcock showers ever again.

"Oh I don't know, I could really work you up into a sweat."

"Well erm, ah." The fly-half ran past them on the way to completing a lap of the pitch and winked at Fiona which was spotted by Ashley.

"Oh yes, what have we here then?" he asked jovially.

"He asked me out."

"Ah love at first sight."

"He's not my type, I prefer my men more cerebral. Plus I don't want to be with someone who spends more time in the mirror than I do."

"And who's the lucky man then?"

"No one at the moment, I broke up with someone a few months back."

"Ah, sorry, well I'm sure there will be another just around the corner." Fiona looked insulted. "Sorry, that came out wrong. I meant you will meet someone nice soon, and they will be a very lucky man, I can tell you." Fiona smiled warmly at the squirming Ashley then Thais walked up with the kids. She'd clocked the physio's look at her husband from a mile out.

"What are you doing here?" asked Ashley.

"Picking kids up. Remember," she snapped. When the children saw her, they ran over and went to hug her. "What I say about get me muddy? Now to car, go." They ran towards the SUV. "And put muddy boots in bag first." She then turned back and her eyes narrowed.

"And who this?"

"This is the new team physio, Fiona meet Thais." They shake hands, but when Fiona went to pull her hand away, Thais held on to it.

"My husband tell me, nothing, about you." she almost hissed as Fiona freed her hand.

"I'm just getting the boys into shape." Owen jogged passed them on lap 2, bulging biceps and his mane flying in the wind. "Just a gentle warm down, always like to do it after a workout," he boasted trying to impress. When Thais saw him, she started to melt.

"Oh, I can see that," she said as she watched him jog towards the changing rooms.

9

Ashley and Thais drove up to the gate where Howley was smoking beside it. He'd been surprised that she wanted to come and was glad she was showing support. The boys were in the back so it was a nice family outing. Ashley got out and Thais continued up the drive. Howley pinned up a printed piece of paper with an arrow and text saying 'Parking'.

"Game day eh Howley."

"Beside myself I am." Ashley lifted up the Badcock sign from the ground.

"We need to get Woody to fix this."

"Who do you think put it up."

"What are the other team like?"

"Better than us."

"I reckon the chaps are going to do this you know."

"Great coming from someone with so much rugby knowledge."

"OK, I may not be an expert, but I like to think I can motivate people. Let's get behind the chaps," Ashley said rousingly.

"It's lads or preferably boys. Chaps hunt or play polo," Howley said. Ashley didn't seem to register that bit of advice or take it in.

"I think you may be wrong coach."

"You'll see."

The opponents for the first game were Haverly-on-Thames (aka The Hoppers for a reason no one knew or cared to ask). Haverly was a very expensive town by the river, full of beautiful houses, beautiful people and lovely families. There were two Michelin Star restaurants, one a pub, the other a full-on pricey fine dining restaurant. They had resisted a Starbucks or Costa for many years because their cafes were far better and run by locals for locals. Eventually, they had to succumb, and when they did, not many of those cafes survived. It was all very well being bouji but that came at a price, one which made their coffee completely un-competitive. The economies of scale and ingredient buying power of the biggies was just too much for them to fight. When the locals were offered something at half the cost, they voted with their wallets, despite the coffee also being half the quality. The sort of town Haverly was had been encapsulated in an Instagram account that became very famous. It was called 'Overheard in Waitrose' and quoted memorable statements from shoppers in that particular upmarket supermarket on Haverly High Street. It detailed such bon mots such as 'Darling, do we need Parmesan for both homes?' and "No marinated artichokes? It's like East Berlin in here." Their club brought about 30 supporters but the difference between them and the Badcock mob couldn't have been starker. The uniform of the Hoppers' gang, called names like Jerome Hinkley-Wallis, was the full-on country kit. A lot of green, tweed, wax jackets, flat caps, cords and wellies. They arrived en masse in SUVs and had brought shooting sticks to sit on during the match. The only shooting sticks Badcock supporters owned, you needed a licence for. There was a wide range of picnics out of the back of said motors with plenty of gin and plonk flowing like water, dished out with raucous bonhomie. Ashley wondered how he lost his licence from one glass over, but these guys were probably going to drive home plastered. Shane summed up BTRFC's effort. He was fully kitted out in knock-off leisurewear and takkies (as Faf called trainers). He had a tab on the go whilst he drank a special brew from the can.

David manned the scoreboard. Beside him, Breeda stood totally uninterested in proceedings behind a trestle table covered in cans of lager and bitter. There were no soft drinks and both types of beverages were warm. They hadn't been able to fit in the small bar fridge beforehand, so she took the executive decision to not bother trying to cool the lager in any way. She had a cash box for anyone who wanted to purchase the beer at £1 per can and it had started filling up. David placed letters and numbers on the scoreboard– a 'H' then a '0', an 'A' then a '0'. The 'A' fell off as soon as he hung it, he left it on the floor.

Howley and Ashley took their places on the sideline. Fiona joined wearing a high vis singlet with the word 'Medic' on the front and back. She was way more medically trained than any of the other coaching staff or indeed anyone at Badcock. Not a hard feat seeing as they couldn't even rustle up a plaster if needed. Just before kick-off, a tall, big-chested man of stature arrived beside them. He wore a fleece with 'Hunt Sewage' printed on the breast, and green wellies.

"Ashley, this is the guy who started this tournament," stated Howley. Michael thrust out his hand enthusiastically.

"Michael Hunt, very pleased to meet you."

"Ashley Havers, likewise."

"But you can call me Mike." Ashley tried his very best to suppress a laugh. "I'm so glad you're here in this little tourney, proper rugby. Well best of luck," Michael said as he wandered off, waiving at people that didn't seem to know him.

In the first ten minutes, Haverly scored a converted try, but the match was really stop-start, mainly because of the penalties given away by Badcock. There were a couple of dust-ups but nothing major. In the Gallagher Premiership, there would have been at least three players in the bin by the 10-minute mark, but this was grassroots rugby, real rugby.

"We're doing all right Howley, you see I told you."

"There's only ten minutes gone man, don't worry, they'll fuck it up." The whistle went for another penalty, this time for Badcock on the Haverly 22. Suddenly Howley took his hands out of the pockets and became more animated than Ashley had seen. He shouted "Jockey 123, Jockey 123" at the players. He turned to Ashley. "Here's one for your bloody tea cups."

"But I wasn't envisaging using it after so little time."

"Trust me, for these boys to even level the scores, no matter at what stage of the match, that's real pressure."

"Let's see what you've come up with then."

They opted to kick for touch instead of going for the points. Shambles actually hit his mark with the middle jumper and Faf received the ball quickly, well quick for them anyway. He sent a good flat pass to Wilkinson who dummied the incoming defender, then threw a missed pass to the wing, Ellis Nowell. The no 11 went left, then right, round the opposing player to score near the posts.

Everyone supporting Badcock was so shocked that their team could put such a move together they forgot to cheer. Howley and Ashley hadn't, they cheered and clapped loudly. Fiona, jumped up in ecstasy, gripping Ashley's forearm as she did. He tried not to react but her grip was so strong, he felt she was ripping his arm off. He really felt sorry for Tiny back when she grabbed his veg. How on earth had he not been hospitalised? David was open-mouthed. Breeda turned to him.

"What the feck? Was that us?" David just nodded still amazed at what he'd just seen. She grabbed a can quickly, opened it and took a huge gulp.

"Well done boys," Howley shouted.

"I say, that was rather good wasn't it?" Ashley asked.

Faf jogged back from celebrating with the guys on the try line. He went very close to the retreating opposing scrum half.

"How about that eh! We're going to tear you all new ones bruh," he said as he jogged past the number 9 whilst the fly-half slotted the extra points.

"Keep your hair on Pikey," the retort came. That remark stopped Faf in his tracks. He ran back to square up to the guy who'd just insulted him. He was at least twice as wide as his opponent but still had to look up, because he was at least three inches shorter. The player mock-laughed and patted him on the head like a child. Faf threw the first punch but completely missed. This was a cue for all teammates from both sides to pile into a big fracas with proper punches being thrown. The referee was in the melee, blowing his whistle repeatedly trying to stop them all. David and Breeda took a selfie with beside the H 7

A 7 scoreboard, Breeda had to hold up the 'A' and both totally ignored the fight. Howley lit up a cigarette.

"Isn't anyone going to stop this?" Ashley asked.

"Just handbags butty bach." The fight ended as quickly as it started with the to number 9s being pulled apart by both sets of players, still trading insults.

That try was the highlight for Badcock in the rest of the half. They were beaten in every aspect of the game, after that. Haverly even ran in a try from their own line just to rub it in. Shambles did his best to live up to his nickname, he hit one of the non-jumping opposing players on the side of the face.

HT Badcock Town 7 Haverly 38

The halftime whistle was seriously needed. All the players trooped off to the changing rooms. They used to just gather on the pitch, with orange quarters, but with the onset of professional rugby, things changed. BTRFC were nowhere near the p in professional, but like many grassroots clubs, seeing all the pros do it, they copied the practice. Ashley stood surveying the scene. He didn't know much about rugby, but he knew this team, the team he now owned, were terrible and the other lot were infinitely better.

10

Fortesque arrived in his Land Rover and pulled by the edge of the pitch where Ashley stood. His grinning face appeared as the window went down.

"What ho!" the Spartan man shouted. Ashley nodded grudgingly. Fortesque saw Fiona standing beside Ashley.

"Fiona, I heard you'd teamed up with this bunch of losers. Why don't you come over to the winning side?" Fiona just stared at him intensely tapping her foot in anger. "Long way back for your boys now Havers."

"It's a game of two halves you know," Ashley protested. He'd heard that phrase in hockey and thought I should transfer OK.

"Yes of course. Anyway, I thought I'd let you know this is the spot where we're just trying to work out if it's the gym or the tennis courts. Toodle pip." He chortled. His tyres spun in the mud as accelerated off, depositing a fine spray over Ashley who was starting to get a Hans level of dislike for that pompous ass.

"What a complete, and utter bastard that man is," Fiona said.

As the team ran out for the second half, everyone there tried to give them a rousing cheer and encouragement. Breeda stayed on her phone, she'd seen it all before so this wasn't new.

"Come on chaps!" shouted Ashley as he clapped and Howley moved beside him. "Lads, come on lads," He corrected himself.

"Can we do this Howley?"

"Not a chance in hell."

"They're not that bad, there's a couple of gooduns in there," Fiona said.

The Hoppers scored four unanswered tries in the second half. The last one summed up how truly awful Badcock were. A high kick was aimed at Robinson back on his 22. As the ball hung there, delusional dad shouted, "Last line of defence son!" The no 15 actually caught it and with the chasers bearing down on him, he tried to clear his lines. With a slice hitherto never seen on a rugby pitch before, it went backwards. The opposing wing ran past him, all he had to do was fall on the ball as it bobbled over the Badcock try line. A first for everyone, an own try.

FT Badcock Town 7 Haverly 62

Ashley sat outside the clubhouse with his head in his hands beside the scoreboard. There was laughter and general noise coming from the bar, the players had long moved on from the game, beer was to be drunk. Howley arrived with two pints and handed one to Ashley who hesitated.

"You will drink this one," The Welshman insisted. Ashley accepted it begrudgingly but still took a number of huge gulps.

"Why did I think I could do this? I'm in PR not a rugby club owner for Christ's sake." Howley sighed. They both looked up at the full-back's dad out on the pitch with him, throwing up a ball with instruction. "He actually kicked the ball backwards," Ashley said despairingly shaking his head.

"He did. Look, I really don't know why I'm doing this."

"You and me both Howley."

"No, telling you that they had a ringer." Ashley kept his head in his hands but didn't react to Howley. "Jesus wept, one of their players is a pro."

"They all looked pros compared to us."

"So they broke the rules." Ashley kept looking at the ground and shrugged. "Which means they should be kicked out of the competition." Finally, the lightbulb moment came for Ashley. "Come inside. Win or lose, you always drink with the team, it's a matter of respect and tradition."

"Even if they're shit?"

"Especially if they're shit."

In the bar pretty much all the firsts, some family and friends plus the committee had stayed and were drinking gallons of beer. So too was Thais, not beer but an absolutely rank white wine that Breeda dug out from the shelves. It could have provided a solution to any energy crisis, but she held it nonetheless, albeit with a face like she was chewing a wasp. Ashley had been shocked when told him she'd come having previously vowed never to step foot in that horrible place with those horrible people. She told him it was to support her husband. They were going to make some serious money on the property deal, and she wanted to help Ashley make it.

Ritchie was spinning the tunes in the corner from the 'DJ Booth'; more 80s music was blasted from the speakers. Despite Ashley's previous pledge, the guy looked as though he was going to jump off a cliff when told he could no longer do it. So Havers relented. Breeda was arm wrestling Budgie and pushed massively with both hands, but budgie's arm stayed perfectly still whilst he drank a pint.

Thais stood over to the side off the bar, talking to Wilkinson. When Ashley pulled up beside her, she readjusted her body position to a more neutral one away from Owen.

"Thanks for being here love, I really appreciate it," Ashley said to Thais when he moved beside her.

"It ok," Thais said whilst smiling at Wilkinson. Ashley turned to Howley.

"We lost badly, why's everyone so happy and drinking like they won?"

"The game's gone, we lost, nothing we can do about that now so we might as well have some fun." He moved into the centre of the room to address everyone. "Now boys, time for dick of the day," he shouted. All the players chant and clap 'Shambles'. "Not this time, he always gets it, so we decided to give it Budgie." All the players chanted 'Budgie' who moved to the middle of the room. He was handed a flower vase of black liquid and proceeded to down it cheered on by all the players.

"What hell is that? Looks like something from the showers," Ashley asked Wilkinson.

"It's a chocolate spider," Wilkinson said.

"Oh do tell, why's that Wilkinson?" Thais asked whilst placing her hand on his arm.

"Because you need eight legs to get home after drinking it." Thais over laughed and touched Wilko's arm again. Ashley's mobile went off and he moved away to answer it. Budgie downed the drink in one go to cheers from all around. Havers finished his call and rushed beside Budgie in the middle of the room.

"Everyone listen up," he shouted.

"What's this idiot want?" came from somewhere in the crowd.

"Haverly fielded a pro, which means they've defaulted and we go through to the next round." The players were silent, looked around at each other and all then cheered throwing drinks up in the air. "And so, our next opponents are Rozzertown."

"Well that's us fucked then," one of the players said.

Ashley and Howley sat in the corner watching the remnants of the soiree. There weren't many people left. Wilkinson was arm wrestling Shambles with Fiona and Thais looking on. Thais had clearly had a drink and was over-enthusiastically cheering Wilkinson on, who only had eyes for Fiona. Ashley was on the Coke Zeros, he agreed to drive because Thais was coming and he had more than learned his lesson. They watched Budgie talking to Breeda over the bar, and it was the unmistakably obvious look of a guy lovestruck. She didn't seem to notice at all.

"So what about Breeda and Budgie?" asked Ashley.

"He's been like a teen trying to get her to the prom for a while now."

"She doesn't seem too interested."

"She knows what she's doing, trust me."

"Why did someone say we're screwed in playing Rozzertown? Sounds like a children's tv programme," Ashley snorted to himself.

"They're coppers," Howley stated.

"Police from Rozzertown, you couldn't make it up,"

"Some say it's where the saying first came from, on account of it being a big Police town back in the day."

"You learn something new every day."

"They're brutal bastards in rugby,' Howley said.

"That's something I wasn't expecting in this day and age."

"They can't raise a finger to anyone in their job like the old days of when I was a lad."

"A good thing."

"If you say so. Everyone these days has a camera in their phones if they did any of that sort of stuff, they'd get caught."

"Of course they will."

"A rugby match is allowed violence for them. It's easy to get digs in and get away with it. Only the referee will sanction them and the standards of our refs in this county is shocking."

"Jesus, sounds like carnage. Do our guys know about his?"

"Of course they do, they've been on the end of it before."

"And they're ok to play them again?"

"A few of them have a couple of scores to settle."

"Christ, I thought rugby was supposed to be a gentleman's game, unlike football."

"Football is a game for gentlemen played by hooligans. Rugby is a game for hooligans played by gentlemen," Howley said picking up a fresh pint that had magically arrived without either of them seeing how. "They're good blokes though, wait til we're here with them afterwards, Shocking." Howley proclaimed.

"So what are your plans to beat them coach?"

"Make them angry."

"That doesn't sound much of a plan."

"Why not?"

"Well correct me if I'm wrong, but I was thinking more about tactics, plays, style of game."

"You're overstepping your mark here." Howley had been slightly angered by Ashley's dismissal of his talents. "You may own this club but last time I looked, I'm the coach." An awkward silence descended until Budgie brought over two tequilas. They were from an alcohol delivery that had fallen off the back of a lorry and as such, had the power to make people sterile. Ashley passed so Howley did them both.

"Listen. When boxers came up against the great Mike Tyson, they always talked a good fight beforehand, how they were going to beat him. Then they always lost. Iron Mike said everyone has a plan until they get punched in the mouth. So that's what we'll do."

"I've done a bit of research on you Howley."

"Google's a wonderful thing. What took you so long?"

"You were tipped to be a Welsh great."

"*Tipped* and *being* are two different things boyo."

"So what happened?"

"You wouldn't understand."

"Try me."

"It's none of anyone's business but my own see. Leave it."

"Come on Howley, you can't just bat me off. How did you end up here?"

"If you're here long enough, you may find out. I won't hold my breath though,"

11

Ashley stood beside Howley on the side of the pitch watching Fiona put the team through the ringer again.

"Rozzertown are bigger, faster, more aggressive and have more skills than us," Howley offered up.

"You really have to work on your pep talks Howley. Inspirational, they are not."

"Bad discipline will get hopefully them."

"Give me a play to do that." Ashley challenged.

"One's called the roundhouse."

"Not very technical, a punch,"

"That was the name for the tables for turning trains around back in the day."

"Oh, right."

"And the move's called that because it starts with the first turn, continues on turning until you have the train facing the other way."

"How?" Ashley couldn't help but be ever so slightly impressed with the coach's initial description, perhaps he did actually have a plan.

"Their tighthead prop is the most likely to go for it. So we wind him up slowly, and constantly, inch by inch, until he snaps, the train turned."

"What will get to him?"

"Oh the usual stuff, a bit of sledging, pisstaking, yah de yah. But we have a secret weapon. We know his wife is divorcing him." They knew this because the wife in question's sister was married to the BTRFC flanker.

"Ah, and how does our guy feel about playing against his soon to be ex brother-in-law."

"Doesn't give a shit, he doesn't like his sister."

"You lot are Eastenders in real life. Where's Bianca?"

"She's our boy's wife."

"I was joking, you know the gobby redhead one from Enders."

"I wasn't."

"Anyway, time to deal with Tarface," Ashley said as he turned and faced the car park. Howley immediately texted Breeda. As he approached the motorhome, a quick glance behind him caught Breeda, Howley and David looking around the outside corner of the clubhouse. They quickly darted back behind the wall in when Ashley turned, only to re-emerge as the owner continued his walk to vehicle on bricks. There was the sound of porn coming from inside and it was rocking slightly. He knocked on the door. The porn noises stopped, as did the rocking. No other sound came from inside.

"Shane, I need to talk to you. Please can you open the door." More silence. "We need to discuss your situation here in the carpark." Silence again, Ashley just waited staring at the door. He moved on to the concrete block acting as a step up to the entrance and placed his ear to the door. The door suddenly flew open outwards, throwing Ashley to the ground. He gathered himself to see Shane in just an open dressing gown, tissue in hand.

"Ah, Shane, sorry." He just shrugged and stared at Ashley in silence. "I think we have to look into your living arrangements here in the car park," he said as he got up rubbing his cheek. Still just stares from Tarface. "I'd like to ask if there was anywhere you can move your motorhome to?"

"Why would I do that?"

"Well just to get it out of the club carpark."

"Why?"

"It's a bit of an eyesore, I just think it might be better located elsewhere."

"Can't"

"Why not?"

"No engine."

"A motorhome with no engine?"

"Yep, bolloxed."

"I could get it fixed for you."

"Still no good."

"Why?"

"I like it here."

"You see, that's precisely the problem. If we're going to progress in this tournament, I'm going to need the space and a more welcoming site." Shane made no attempt to close his robe and stepped down out of the van. He moved up close to Ashley which brought his appendage into view. Ashley didn't mean to - or want to - but he got a glimpse of why Shane got his nickname. It reminded him of the frostbite he saw once when attempting (and failing) to climb Everest for charity. As well as underwear, deodorant was not Shane's friend. Trying not to gag at the smell, and the sight, Ashley at least stood his ground as Shane came right up to his face.

"I've been here for years. You've been here months. I think I've got more rights." He stared at Ashley, who's eyes were starting to water now as he held down the urge to vomit all over Shane, something he imagined wouldn't go down to well with him.

"Ok, we'll discuss this later," Ashley said as he beat a hasty retreat backwards Mr Bean stylie. He tripped up on a block of concrete with a pole in it that clearly served no purpose whatsoever. As he rolled a few times forward, he ended up face down in a huge puddle. This had existed since anyone at the club could remember, even in Summer. No one had bothered to get it seen to. Ash heard belly-aching laughter from behind the corner where the other three were.

Ashley found Fiona in the clubhouse as he returned from his encounter with Tarface.

"We do have toilets here you know," she said as she looked at Ash's chinos, wet from his crotch down.

"He's a menace that man, and I'm not talking about his haircut." Fiona had been called over by the other three and had witnessed the whole thing. She was trying desperately not to laugh.

"He was really sweet when a drunk guy was all over me after the first game. He got rid of him."

"That guy'll turn up in a hundred years at the bottom of the Thames wearing cement boots."

"Oh I think you're exaggerating Ashley, he's harmless."

"Harmless as the plague – and smells like it. I'm going to dry off." He went off to the gents and tried using the hand dryer. Of course, being Badcock, it only blew out cold air which was useless in the trouser drying stakes, so he decided to jack that idea in after a couple of minutes. This ensured he was irritated when he came back.

"So you're a social media influencer?" he asked Fiona after a cup of rosy. Since being at the club, he'd found a healing quality to builders' tea. Much to Thais' horror, he insisted on a box of Yorkshire tea bags in the house. Of course, there were no tea plantations in Yorkshire bar the ones mixing up a brew fashioned from the magic mushrooms plentiful on the moors. Ashley had been picking mm once on the other moor, Dartmoor, when visiting a friend at Plymouth University. As the group found a particularly plentiful patch, they were interrupted. An army search and rescue helicopter using the terrain for training, hovered above the hapless group. The instant reaction was to throw the corner shop plastic bags of freshly picked shrooms to the ground. Nothing to see there. As young'uns, they had no idea the army could do precisely zero about their booty and would have joined them if they could. Ashley saw both pilots clear as day, laughing hysterically at a bunch of stupid students panicking about something they'd picked that grew naturally and available to everyone. He continued, "I know all about these guys of course, it is my business after all."

"Oh yes, please impart your knowledge oh wise one."

"A lot of them do it because they're either thick as pigshit or simply can't do anything else. They took the easy way out. Why work when you can flash your teeth in a badly shot video to the delight of other stupid people. Then there are the ones who come from money but feel being an influencer is a worthwhile way of them showing they're not vacuous morons." Ashley realised his irritation at Shane had now manifested itself in front of Fiona. She looked taken aback. He'd been building those thoughts up for a while having dealt with so many social media stars in his work, but wasn't expecting to unleash them at her, definitely not at her.

"I wasn't born with a spoon in my mouth, unlike some. I have worked hard to get what I've got. Yes, I have celeb clients. Yes I'm on socials a bit but all it's about the hustle. That's not the world I grew up with, nor want. It's my job Ashley. If I can get an edge any way over the other guys, to drive demand for my books and classes, then why not?" It was a rhetorical question. This had gone rapidly south, and he needed to rescue it.

"Well I am very glad you're here. It's going to make all the difference."

"Even though I'm supposedly thick as pigshit."

12

In the changing room, the team sat in their matchday kit. Faf was doing the talk, aggressively.

"Got in their fucking heads man. Get the first tackle in, even if it's late. Get them so fucking wound up, they want to rip your heart out with a spoon. Any chance you get, give them the verbals. All the tricks boys. They will lose it man." They all shouted Badcock in unison with one clap when Faf finished.

Ashley came in holding a big brown box, grinning from ear to ear.

"So boys, I've got us a sponsor." He announced jubilantly as he dumped the box in the middle of the floor. "They're a builder's merchants in Badcock. Go on, grab your kit," he said as pointed at the box. The players started pulling out the kit from the box. Budgie held up a shirt that had his name and the number 4 on the back. On the front, it said in huge letters 'Ivor Biggun'. Then he pulled out the shorts and across the backside was also the same name.

"Supposedly it's all the rage seeing as people see a lot of your arses during a game." Many of the players laugh hysterically. The name of this merchant had long been a local joke but now Ashley wanted to make them part of the merriment.

"I'm not fucking wearing that," Faf said as he pulled out his shirt and shorts.

"You have to, it's our new sponsor."

"No way bruh. You can shove that shirt and those shorts right up your arse man." Taking his lead, all the players throw the kit they had just picked up, on the floor. The Ivor Biggun sponsorship deal (a very small amount) was abandoned there and then. They all ran out in their old kit.

Rozzertown bought along quite a few supporters but the thing that stuck out was that they included officers in uniform that were on duty for 'public safety reasons'. That was the official line but there had never been a police presence needed or requested at a Badcock game, so they were clearly on the skive to watch the match. When their radios crackled with various chatter, they never acknowledged them once. Badcock had managed a turnout of decent proportions by their standards. Ashley had told all the players to make sure they had at least one friend or family member come along. All those f & f had in the past always found an excuse to not stand on a cold muddy sideline to watch a truly terrible rugby team get beaten every time. There were always far better things to do, like having their kidneys removed. But Ashley promised any supporter free beer for turning up and nothing focuses the resolve like the offer like that. So they had around 40 which was a really good turnout for them. When Ashley gave the players the offer, he missed off the 'a' and so it got translated to their loved ones as 'free beer'. As such, the few 'towners' that turned up, expected to be replenished with ale like they were on an all-inclusive holiday in Torremolinos. Ashley had to relent when the first ten to arrive (3 hours before kick-off) expected their 2nd one as part of the promised package. Their mood turned ugly when Breeda laid down the law.

"It's only one feck'n beer morons. You have to pay for any more," she shouted at them as they started to rant and rave as though they'd already had a whole day on the lash. David spotted it could turn ugly and called Ashley.

"These guys have been promised free beer all day."

"Who promised them that?"

"You."

"I did no such thing. I said to the players a beer. One beer. Singular."

"They're expecting more and if you don't give it to them, they could get troublesome."

"Luckily we've got the police around then."

62

"They'll be more likely to join in."

"I've never heard such a thing."

"The guys are Shane's friends."

"But he's not even here."

"If you don't give them free beer, be careful going home tonight. They would see it as a man breaking his word, and that doesn't go down very well." Ashley looked over at the group of tattooed bodybuilders wearing wife beaters and remonstrating with Breeda. He knew he couldn't put her in that position. So, the supporters were replenished sufficiently, and expensively. When the Rozzertown supporters found out about this magic alcohol tap, they too demanded the same. Ashley had to come up with a ruse whereby it appeared that Badcock supporters/members had pre-paid at a club discounted rate and so there was no such thing as free beer, for anyone. It just about worked.

It was the first time Shane could not be seen in the carpark, or indeed anywhere. Ashley thought his little chat with the mulleted one had been successful. It was explained to him though that the Rozzertown team and their supporters made Shane nervous and thought it wise to not risk anything unpleasant like being arrested. So just not being there was his go-to play.

As their team ran on the pitch, Ashley recognised two of the players, they were the officers Howley spoke to when they arrived at the rave.

"Is it me or are Police getting smaller?" Ashley asked.

"The true sign of old age, the police are getting shorter."

The Rozzertown boys lived up to their reputation. Within 20 minutes, they had two players in the sin-bin at the same time. They went into halftime with another on the naughty step. They still managed to be better than Badcock, even with all the yellow cards.

HT Badcock Town 6 Rozzertown 9

Although this was just a Hunt tourney game, the referee was

being as harsh as the fiercest international referees officiating the World Cup final. Their manager approached the referee as they walked close to Ashley and Howley on the sideline as the players went into the sheds.

"What the hell are you doing? You're letting these guys get away with murder but penalising my guys without cause," he shouted.

"I'm being fair; your guys are committing too many fouls, dangerous play, and downright nasty digs."

"I'm not a great reader of the subtleties of rugby discipline," Ashley whispered to Howley.

"No shit."

"But even I know that referee seems to be on our side, big time. It's not a fair competition."

"If we rile up a few more, they could go too."

"You keep going on about the ethics of rugby, shouldn't we say something? Isn't that part of your precious code?"

"Listen, the ref's brother got sent down for car theft and one of the guys that arrested him was from this force. It's fair to say he's on our side."

"Isn't that unfair?"

"Is it fuck boyo. Keep it zipped."

At 70 minutes in, with the scores level, one of the Rozzertown props punched Shambles in the face after they squared up from a collapsed scrum. Thompson just laughed sarcastically at the puncher in a way that would have made Ali proud. That was an immediate red, leading to uncontested scrums and suddenly the game became relatively easy for the smurfs. They actually scored a converted try (courtesy of Budgie) and hung on from there.

FT Badcock Town 13 Rozzertown 12

A few Rozzertown players joined everyone in the bar. There were the two officers from the rave, and another two. To Ashley's surprise, so were two of the uniformed officers (one WPC) who'd been standing on the sidelines. They had pints in their hands.

"Shouldn't they be sober on duty?" Ashley asked Howley.

"They're off duty now," he said. "Now perk up boyo, this is where it gets interesting," Everyone was slow clapping and cheering. Four BTRFC players moved into the centre of the room and turned their backs to the uniformed WPC who stood facing them. Then the players bent over. The WPC removed the bright yellow taser from her belt to rapturous applause and cheering by all present.

"What's she doing with that?" Ashley asked, slightly horrified at the implications of a taser with a load of drunk people.

"Wait," he said then shouted out "2!" Everyone else started shouting numbers to Faf who wrote them down in a notebook. Budgie approached the WPC with a bar towel in his hand to more cheering and numbers being shouted. He smiled, bowed and then tied the towel around her head covering her eyes. The officer was spun round once to face the prone backsides. Budgie withdrew with ceremony. She raised the taser at them and the crowd counted down from three. On fire, she pulled the trigger releasing the barbs at the derrieres. They hit the second guy in line who collapsed convulsing from the volts coursing through his body. Everyone cheered. The WPC removed the towel and went to help the now-prone player who was so drunk, he barely even felt it.

"It's always number two," Howley said. "That'll be ten quid from Faf." Ashley was appalled.

"This is so wrong on so many levels Howley," Ashley said.

"Don't worry, he too gets fifty."

"This has to stop."

"There's only one more go, don't worry, they have turned the voltage down, it's not dangerous."

"No. There is no way this should be happening."

"Do you want to tell them?" Howley gestured towards a bunch of very large drunks and a WPC with a taser. "We can have the inquiry tomorrow Mr PR. OK?" Ashley nodded grudgingly, he wasn't going to take on everyone there in the state they were in, including the police, off duty or not. This time, the taser operator was shambles who could hardly stand up as it was. Some of the audience backed away but still, one person, amazingly, replaced the previous number two in the line.

He was spun around by Budgie, but when the big fella let him go, Shambles continued spinning, fell over and as he hit the ground, discharged the taser. Ashley can only remember the searing second of more pain than he'd ever encountered in his life before he passed out. He came around as the WPC and Howley wafted towels to try and help revive him. Everyone else was still having fun totally ignoring the medical drama. Faf handed out cash to the punters, he ran a very tidy book.

13

The committee watched in silence as Ashley placed a paracetamol jar on the table, a water bottle and then a few other jars of pills. He stared at Howley with scorn as he placed each one down. The Welshman looked sheepish.

"That one is for my allergies," Ashley said, pausing for effect. "I hadn't had them for years." He opened the jar slowly, took the pills out, screwed the cap on and stared at Howley again. He picked up another jar, did the same and said, "Those are for my back, again not had troubles in years."

"Ashley..." the coach said but was stopped by Havers raising his hand.

"That was until an utterly shit hooker, so pissed he didn't know his own name, who can't throw a fucking rugby ball to save his life, was given a fifty-thousand-volt taser. It doesn't take a fucking genius to grasp the insanity of that action," Ashley paused for effect. "But these pills testify to my initial hunch at the time that it was a fucking stupid idea." They hadn't heard Ashley swear before, and it only added to the naughty boy shame they were feeling. David broke the resultant silence.

"That's the first time something like that has ever happened. I don't think we'll have that ever again Ashley." They could hear Breeda laughing, again like some ghostly presence.

"Please don't drop the cops in it. They would lose their jobs," Howley stated.

"My wife's on the board of a Police charity, so the last thing I'll do is drop them in it just because some arseholes thought it a great idea to give an even bigger arsehole a weapon." Again, there was sheepish silence. Ashley didn't really need the pills, his back was fine, and allergies had stayed away, but he wanted to make a point to them. It would help when he tried to put his foot down if they were more compliant.

"Ok, we move on," he said, changing the direction and mood. David wanted to bring up the fact they lost money because of the free beer stunt but thought better of it considering the mood of the owner. "The ringer in the first game gave me an idea, let's get one of our own for the next game." This brought the members back into normal service.

"What do you know about ringers in rugby?" David asked.

"I know that if we could get one, we'd have a better chance of winning."

"You don't think there are people in this room that know more about rugby players, and who they play for, than you?" Howley had moved from sheepish to insulted. "If there were a way for us to get one, you don't think we would have done it already?"

"You never got this one." Ashley unlocked his phone and pulled up a picture. It was of a smiling handsome man with arms crossed, a black background and the French Rugby logo in the top corner. The man was wearing a French international senior men's team kit. He showed it to Howley who burst out laughing.

"Yeah right boyo. Badcock Town RFC, who play non-league grassroots rugby in a shithole is getting Serge Sella, French centre and one of the superstars of French and world rugby. Brilliant plan Ashley." Everyone looked at each other and smirked mockingly. Ashley hit facetime on his phone and after hearing a foreign ringtone on the speaker, they heard "Allo".

"Hi Serge. I'm with some of the Badcock committee, and they want to say hello." Ashley showed the phone screen to Howley and David who could only wave pathetically at an image of the smiling Frenchman, this time live, complete with cows roaming in a field behind him, his cows.

"Allo gentlemen. I look forward to playing for you guys and meeting you all."

"Thanks Serge, I'll give you a call later." Ashley hung up the phone and placed it back on the table. He delayed looking up as he rustled around his bag for effect. When he did, their jaws were still on the floor, staring at him. "What do you think guys, he'll do right?"

"There's no way he will be allowed to play in the tournament," David said.

"Why's that?" Ashley asked.

"He's a fucking French international for one, people might just notice that," Howley scoffed.

"Ex-French international," Ashley jumped in.

"What?"

"Oh didn't you hear? He's given up."

"Either way, there is dim siawns he will be allowed to play."

"I really need a translator on hand. The rules of the tournament are very clear–no professional players. He's not professional, he got out of professional rugby."

"He's a Six Nations and World Cup winner for fuck's sake, why the hell is he coming to play here, and how do you know him?" Howley questioned. Ashley wasn't going to tell them the truth, he needed kudos around the place and this was going to provide it. What had actually happened was the use of Josh's encyclopaedic and near-fanatic rugby brain. He played a video simulation game where he was the manager of England senior side. All data on teams around the world and players from every rugby playing country, were updated in real time. Every single stat and worldwide rugby story were fed into the game's algorithm. Serge cropped up after he confided in an obscure French rugby journalist. Sella had grown disillusioned with the international and professional game. He came from Bayonne in Southwest France. They eat, drink and sleep rugby, it's in their genes. It was claimed that when babies were born in the town, the midwives would cut the umbilical cord and then rugby pass the newborn into the crib. The grassroots game was more important to them than any of the fancy stuff. A match was a time when they could share saucisson and glass of red with friends whilst watching some great rugby.

Josh had met Sella a few years before he was a superstar. He went to an England A side vs France A. He ended up in a

bar near the ground where Serge was with a few friends. Josh
had been following Sella's career, admired his play and wanted
to get a selfie with the young Frenchman. He obliged but then
when the two started talking rugby, they hit it off. They became
friends, although Josh had no idea about Serge's intentions until
he was notified about the story. When they spoke about it, Josh
hatched a plan. Serge still wanted to play grassroots rugby and
had always liked the English game. When Josh asked him about
joining Badcock, he went for it. Josh didn't tell him that instead
of great wine, food, cows, and maybe a fragrant cheese, rugby
at Badcock was raw, and the townsfolk were usually in the dock
rather than a rugby ground. The star saw it as a challenge. It
would be a few games, he'd get to have a laugh, and so what. He'd
stay in a nice hotel in London and see a lot friends.

"French right?" Ashley said when Josh said he'd secured the
services of Sella.

"What you, of all people, know of him?" Ash had taken a
guess, he wasn't going to be Scottish with that name.

"Not a clue." None of this was going to be divulged to the
committee staring at Ashley.

"Well, in my PR career, I have had to cold call a lot. Now
that I'm a club owner, I'm reading the rugby press. There were
rumours about Serge wanting to give it all up. So I got his
number and called him up. I speak French and he was very nice.
End of story really."

"Fuck me!" Howley said. Breeda's voice came from the ether
again, "Oh my fucking good god. Yes, yes. Whoo-hoo"

"He's not going to be with us until after the next game, so
who've we got?" Asked Ashley.

"Merthyr Town Miners," David piped.

"First, Merthyr is in Wales"

"And in this county." Howley said, sighing heavily

"Second, there are no mines, Welsh or otherwise, in Berkshire.
Plus you're the first red dragon I've met in the area, so I'm
guessing it's not much of a diaspora."

"Whatever that is, the miners' families came here from

Merthyr, including my family, when the pits closed down. They pulled names out of a hat and Berkshire came up first."

"What are they like as a team?"

"We're not going to win."

"That's not the spirit I was hoping for Howley."

"Just being realistic. My brother has the inside track."

"You're kidding! Why haven't I heard about your flesh and blood?"

"We don't talk."

"You don't talk to your brother who even lives in the same county. That's madness."

"You know nothing about our family and why me and Gethin are not exactly bosom buddies."

"When was the last time you talked?" Howley shifted around in his seat uncomfortably.

"Er, well, 3 years."

"That's insane and very sad. What caused the bust up?"

"Barry John."

"What?"

"I knew you wouldn't know him."

"You both knew this guy?"

"No."

"So how does this Barry cause you and your brother not to talk?"

"We'd had a few beers. It was Wales v England in the Six Nations, and we were in Cardiff after the match. We got on to the greatest Welsh player of all time. I said Barry John, he said Gareth Edwards."

"I fail to see how that would lead to you both not talking to each other."

"Well it got a bit tasty see. We went outside. I can't remember who threw the first punch. Then there were some other boys looking for a scrap and so they joined in. Once it was all over, we went our separate ways, and that was it."

"That is easily the crappest reason for not speaking to your brother I've ever heard."

"We take Welsh rugby very seriously."

"No kidding. Jesus, my children have more sense."

"Well, that was until today."

"Excellent, why's that?"

"He's the Miners' coach."

"The boys will front up," Ashley said. "I know it. Set-piece and aggression will get us over the line." Howley raised an eyebrow, not this time in contempt but in recognition of Ashley's adaptation.

Game day vs Merthyr. Ashley found Howley smoking outside the clubhouse. A bandy-legged man in a tracksuit arrived beside them both. Although the spitting image of Howley facially, he had no hair whatsoever. His pate was shiny and round looking like an egg with eyes, but apart from that, every other characteristic was the same. The deep crevices in the skin, disarming blue eyes set into the cliff-face visage, a gait that could stop a pig in an alleyway, all traits marking them out as twins. The siblings didn't even shake hands, just a nod.

"Geth," Howley said through his teeth without looking at him.

"How," Gethin acknowledged. Ashley looked from brother to brother and back again, astounded by the fact that these were the first words either man had spoken to each other in three years.

"Really guys?" Ashley asked. The men stayed stoic and stared straight ahead.

"Gethin, I'm Ashley, owner of Badcock." They shook hands.

"Well he's no Jockey." Geth said to his brother.

"True that." Howley acknowledged.

"I see the social skills of a rock run in the family." They both huffed and sighed, still looking at the pitch, kicking at the mud. Gethin's mobile rang. He didn't say much when he answered and there was no conversation. He nodded and Ashley heard what sounded like Welsh coming out of the phone. Geth then hung up without any acknowledgement, turned and walked off to the carpark.

"Game's off," Howley said as he too turned and made off towards the clubhouse.

"What? Mind telling what that was?"

"Their team bus has broken down and they won't make it here in time. Forfeited game."

"Where'd you get that from?"

"Cousin Evan, he was the guy on the other end of the phone."

"He was loud, didn't need a phone really."

"A fine baritone in his day, I tell you. He's known as the foghorn."

"And what's he got to do with this little drama from the valleys?"

"He's their driver."

It emerged later that Shane's dodgy work had a hand in the breakdown. The mulletted one had taken helping the club to win, as a personal mission. He broke into the miner's car park and put sugar into the petrol tank. Badcock through to the next round.

14

Serge was staying at the *Montrose*, a traditional French rugby hotel, i.e. it was usually where the team stayed when playing England at Twickenham. All international teams had their own preferences and criteria for choosing where to stay. England always preferred something nearer the stadium they were playing at and, if they could, out of the city centre. This was particularly true in Wales or Scotland where the bevvied up pesky locals would do their best to keep the team awake with as much noise in the street as possible. The French preferred the *Montrose* in London because it had a Michelin star chef who happened to be a rugby fan, so would always serve them up a personalised feast when they were guests. Serge knew the manager, and after a call, he was basically offered the keys to the hotel at a fraction of normal costs.

Some young female French inhabitants of London had found out their hero was staying there. Ashley waited outside and as Serge exited, the group screamed, and surged forward with phones for selfies. The autograph had long disappeared as young peoples' methods of getting a keepsake from their heroes. Serge wasn't taken aback and obliged the ten or so fans with selfies in various forms. He thanked them, saw Ashley out of the car waving, and headed over to him, still grinning that famous French grin that had made him a fortune off the pitch. Usually it was the footballers who had all the contracts for high-end watchmakers, aftershave, cars and underpants. He was a brands' wet dream. Good looking, athletic, wholesome but also bright, he wanted to be a doctor before rugby took over his life, erudite and very humble. Serge had been ranked as the highest endorsement earning star in France.

When he came out Ashley couldn't help but admire how cool he looked. All in black, with white sneakers. Although he did have a man bag, he carried it off with effortless cool. Ashley hoped it didn't give Thais any ideas. He would have to draw the red line over that one like he had done with the European ball bags briefs instead of swimming shorts. They had a hearty handshake and his genuine manner and warmth was immediately evident.

Thais had approached the soiree like a bridezilla. She too didn't know about him until Google helped. Following hours of painstaking research, many calls to her friends, telling them to use the eponymous search engine just to make them jealous. She knew even less about rugby than Ashley, but she did know celeb culture and the power it can bestow on mere mortals. Surprisingly, Ashley had input to the guestlist for the shindig, but he didn't have a veto, so Hans was in, much to his chagrin. Fiona was the only one from the club to be invited. She'd been given strict instructions not to mention it to anyone at the club. He didn't want people to find out they were NFI and have to deal with that. She was OK to come because she wouldn't judge him on their very nice house, even though it was mortgaged to the hilt. Howley or David would scowl, make assumptions, and it would get back to everyone at the club. He'd somehow be given the status of a royal there, something he didn't like. It was best left alone. Apart from anything else, Ashley wanted her there. The admission on the guest list was surprising because although Thais could win Olympic gold for flirting, she didn't like anyone doing it with her husband.

She was a terrible cook so a friend recommended a French chef who would come to the house and cook for them. He'd do a range of canapes that would knock everyone's socks off. Ashley questioned her sanity when he got the answer to the question, 'How much is this chef costing?' She assured him it would be worth it because Serge would feel at home. She didn't know Serge's favourite type of food was the rustic comfort food from the region he grew up in. If she'd gone to one of the many French delis in London, she could have got some fantastic breads, various charcuterie, cheese and Serge would have been like one of his pigs wallowing in the manure.

When they approached the front door, it was thrown open by Thais.

"Serge," she proclaimed as if he were an old friend. She did an exaggerated double kiss.

"Serge, this my wife, Thais."

"Enchante mademoiselle," he said like the smooth man who used to advertise Gitane cigarettes back in the day. There was a collective silent sigh from the women gathered in clumps around the room.

"Come with me, I'd like to introduce you to some friends," she said as she grabbed his arm and nearly yanked it out of its socket.

"It's good to see him, he's a top bloke," Josh said to Ashley as they surveyed the large sitting room where all were gathered.

"He seems to have quite a fan club," Ashley said observing the Frenchman surrounded by the audience of women.

"You've seen him play right."

"Sure, clips. He seems to score a lot."

"He's a machine and that's at international level, imagine what he'll do in the shit tourney to a load of unfit binmen."

"Thais seems to have taken to the rugby idea," Josh said as Thais moved Serge around like a chess piece.

"How do you mean?"

"Well Badcock is hardly her natural habitat but she might now be visiting a few times."

Ashley had managed to avoid Hans all night. He had nothing to say to him other than 'Hi, how are you?' A rhetorical question that should normally elicited a standard response. It was more a greeting than an actual question. What always happened in Hans' case was he went straight into the deal he was currently working on without even a hint of asking back. 'Totally insane' would be the first words then off he'd go on about how busy he was, how important he was and what a complete c u next tuesday he was. Ashley couldn't avoid him when getting a new bottle of fizz out of the fridge. He closed the door to reveal the shy and retiring dealmaker.

"You know how busy I am, but I have put in some work on your little project."

"Of course you are. What project?"

"Selling the club." Ashley looked around to see where Fiona was, luckily there was no sign. In fact she didn't make it at all because of illness.

"Ok, thanks."

"You've got yourself a real little goldmine there you know." Ashley knew the land might have been worth a bit but hadn't really done the numbers on it. He wanted to enquire further but it was Hans. Through teeth so gritted they almost broke he asked for more. Hans had a property developer who was prepared to pay tens of millions for it. On hearing that, he tried to act cool. He twisted the bottle of champagne to release to the cork.

"Oh, that's quite good." This figure was beyond his wildest imagination. He was in PR not property and would have valued the plot at a few hundred grand. Luckily his kids' futures weren't reliant on his property skills. After everyone had gone home, the place had been left spotless by the guys helping them. Ashley and Thais stood in the kitchen with the last of a bottle of champagne.

"Serge enjoy. I know some of girls liked," she said.

"Not just the girls eh?"

"He smooth."

"I noticed," Ashley said but Thais ignored the insinuation.

"Fiona, really at club?"

"What do you mean?"

"Celebrity fitness trainer and them."

"She wants to do something real, not the sort of thing that your friends would pay a fortune for."

"Why do you always bring it back to this?"

"I'm just saying that appearances, especially in this social media world, are not always what they seem to be. Your lot are all about appearance."

15

Ashley tried to sneak Serge into the club to spring his surprise on the team. The people that knew about his arrival, had decided that they weren't going to tell anyone because a) they didn't believe it themselves and b) no-one else would believe them. The pisstake would be horrific. What Ashley didn't count on was Breeda being a superfan. She'd been to the Aviva stadium in Dublin to watch Ireland take on France in the six nations. Serge ripped into them and the French clinched the title by destroying the men in green. As they got out of the car, she ran up to it from the clubhouse entrance gripping a ruby ball. She wanted it signed to send to her father who'd taken her to that match. Despite him swearing that 'Ireland were playing like 'feck'n shitters' he did say it was a privilege to see such class.

"I'm going to marry that man one day," Breeda said to her father as she looked wistfully at Serge leaving the field after the international.

"Sure love, we'll get the Pope to do the ceremony," her dad commented.

"Mr, mr, ..." Words failed her, she stumbled and stuttered then realised there was only one thing to do. She just thrust out the ball and sharpie pen. Serge smiled and did the business.

"This is Breeda, she runs the bar here, and if you hadn't noticed, she's a massive fan."

"I saw you in Dublin," she just about got out. "You feck'n stuffed us." He flashed that smile as he signed the ball. She almost looked as though she had curtseyed.

"Welcome to our little club," she spluttered.

"I'm looking forward to it," Serge said cheerfully.

The team were in the changing rooms getting a talking to

from Howley about how the training session was going to go. That was a first for them, instructions as to how to train. Usually, the coach opened a bag of balls and told them to get on with it. He would then retire to the bench outside the clubhouse to observe their progress whilst chain smoking. They made up their own routines which were half-heartedly applied at best. Ashley asked Serge to wait outside the door as he bounded in.

"What ho lads!" he shouted.

"Bertie," shouted a number of players. They'd taken to calling him Bertie Wooster, but it went over Ashley's head. Howley wondered if he was ever going to understand how to talk to players without them extracting the Michael.

"Listen, I've got a bit of a surprise for you."

"You're off on a spiffing adventure?" Faf quipped with more laughter following.

"Er, no." Ashley shook his head as if the South African had said something stupid. "We've got a new player joining us."

"Whoo-hoo," they mocked.

"Gentlemen, please welcome him," Ashley said as he flung open the changing room door to reveal Serge in a tracksuit kit bag slung over his hefty shoulders. He walked in, beaming ear-to-ear. Of course, everyone in the team knew exactly who he was. Three of them dropped their drinks. A few more swore with open, mouths. Faf just laughed out loud.

"Yah right brah. Where's Ant and the other one. Hidden camera yah," he said still laughing hard.

"Allo all," the Frenchman said as he made his way to an empty spot on the bench, beside Budgie who was staring like he'd seen a ghost. Serge pointed. "Ok here?" he asked. The big man nodded in awe-struck silence.

"This is Serge Sella, I'm sure some of you will be aware who he is," Ashley said as he took the top prize for stating the bleed'n obvious. Anyone who watched rugby, liked rugby or played rugby, knew who he was. "He's going to play with us for the rest of the tourney." The Frenchman just smiled and nodded. There was shock around the changing room. When they accepted, they weren't the butt of some candid camera prank, it then became clear why Howley had been talking about working around the 10/12 axis a few moments before. He knew what was coming.

"So as I was saying, on that axis– if we can work around Wilkinson and Serge, they can run the midfield, and the forwards support them," he explained with crosses on the chalkboard. That was another event in itself, the only time it ever got used before was for writing rude messages or drawing penises.

"Or what about this, we just give it to Serge every time and watch him score," pipped up Wilkinson.

"Gentlemen," Serge said as everyone listened with the attention of being spoken to by God. "I am here to play with a team, with you guys. This is not about me. Although I may have been playing for France up to now, I am here at bad cock," the way he said it made it sound funny with too much emphasis on the cock. "We're all going to win a tourney together. Rugby is about playing for each other. Every match, every tackle, every kick, every moment we're out on that pitch. OK?" The players nodded like dogs, a couple clapped and Faf let out an over-exaggerated roar that seemed out of place. Ashley felt proud, and Howley was emboldened. He continued to talk about some of the plays they were going to train with today.

Ashley walked out of the changing room behind the team as they ran out with more energy than some of them had mustered in the past decade on anything. They ran past Fiona with Serge bringing up the rear. Ashley sidled up to her all chuffed, chest out and feeling pleased with himself in his acquisition.

"Is he more your type?"

"He is really nice."

"Oh yes?" Ashley asked, fishing. It was none of his business who Fiona was attracted to or not but he found himself more than interested.

"But I don't think his girlfriend would approve."

"What girlfriend?"

"She's an actress in France, she flies comes over to London every month for a training session with me."

"Bloody small world. So you know him already?"

"Never met him before, have you met your wife's trainers?" She had a point, only once did Ashley meet one of the many trainers his wife has utilised in the past, and the fitness guru made him feel wholly insignificant in the muscles department. Fiona jogged off to join the team as Ashley got a call from Fortesque.

"I hear you're bringing in a ringer Havers."

"I don't know what you're talking about Smythe." Ashley had succumbed to the toff's way of calling someone by their surname. It was a military and boarding school thing and a sign of disrespect for the person being named.

"There's a certain international training with you today."

"Again, lost on me."

"Don't play silly buggers with me. I have friends there, people who give me information. I know for a fact that Serge fucking Sella is training there right now." The player had only just been introduced to the team. How did someone in the time between the introduction and running out on the pitch, call Fortesque. "You're pathetic Havers. If you think you're going to play wonder boy in the tournament, believe me, you won't. Just give up and we can get this over sooner rather than later." Ashley hung up.

Havers walked through the carpark to be met by the glorious sight of Shane in his Y-fronts, even though the thermometer said it was only 4 degrees.

"Awight," Shane said as he lit a cigarette.

"Any news on fixing your motorhome?"

"Nope."

"What did the garage say?"

"Can't get the parts."

"How about even some wheels so we can tow it somewhere?"

"Supply chain issues." Shane wouldn't have known what a supply chain was unless it was explained to him in more understandable ways. Family buy TV. Burglar steals TV. Thief sells it to fence for cash to buy drugs. When the stash is all used up, rob house again to get more cash. The supply chain complete. Ashley had discussed offering to buy Shane some wheels but Breeda just laughed at him when he suggested it.

"He's got feck'n wheels, the gobshite just doesn't want to move. You'll never get him to either, just give up," was her sage advice.

Ashley watched the training. The presence of Serge had an effect he wasn't expecting. It seemed as though everyone was just trying a little harder. There was more of everything– shouting, directions, effort, moan groans macho one-on-ones. This was especially true with the two alphas in the group, Faf and Wilkinson. They were giving each other instructions, complaining when something didn't work. The team were still useless but Serge seemed happy to be running around an awful pitch with real amateurs–in name and nature. Howley joined him at the sideline.

"What's the plan coach?"

"We play as a team."

"That's good."

"All the team gets the ball to Serge."

16

Round 4's opponents were previous winners Smitherwick RFC. Another wealthy town that had the honour of having the most expensive houses in the county. It hadn't always been like that. There was an old town and a new one. The old one had a number of pubs that dated back to Henry IV. They were black beamed, thatched roofed with very low doors due to the customers being a lot shorter in those days. They always caught out unsuspecting punters barrelling though at speed. There had been so many cracked head that the edges of door arches had to have cushioned padding put on them. They couldn't knock through the doorways because the local council deemed them historical treasures and so never granted planning permission to do so. They weren't the ones banging their heads. With all the lawyers in the area, if the pubs didn't mitigate the inevitable smashed craniums, they'd be sued to oblivion.

The new town cropped up. It was all tastefully done, there were new build mansions off all the various previously single-track country lanes, many out of the reach of anyone who used to live in the old town. With the introduction of this new part, including a high-end supermarket, restaurants, cafes and cinema, the prices of property in the old town went through the roof. When a high-speed rail link to London was put in, the whole area (old and new) became the most expensive place to live in the country never mind just the county.

Their rugby club was well-funded, well subscribed and well-equipped. They had minis, senior men 1sts, 2nds, 3rds, U16s, vets, and a women 1sts and girls teams. They had 8 pitches at their disposal and their training facilities were Premiership standard. They had produced four of the current England senior men and five of the senior women teams. Their alumni had won world cups, premierships and championships. To say they were a good outfit was ever so slightly underestimating it. They played in the league but used the Hunt tournament to give a run out to the lads, who were basically the unofficial 6ths, if ever such thing could exist. Most of the guys were just old enough, but because they were not professional, not part of the professional set-up at the club, the complied with the tournament rules. They were red hot favourites to smash Badcock into oblivion and out of the competition.

Badcock were playing away and had never met them before on the pitch nor been to their club. Their minibus had broken down so there was a refugee feel to their journey and arrival at their opponents. Shane had managed to borrow another form of transport best described as one the first ever people movers. The rest of the team were crammed into various cars that looked as though they'd been in a battle. New Range Rovers they were not. Ashley drove with Serge, a fawning Breeda in the back and Howley.

As they drove through lush countryside, fields and greenery as far as they eye could see. This for a place that was twenty five minutes from London, no wonder it was an expensive place to live. The entrance to the club had a grand walled and gated front with a buzzer.

"It's like fucking Harry Potter," one of the players remarked as their transport pulled up.

Shane leant out of the window but couldn't reach the buzzer, so opened the door to give himself more room. As he leant on it reaching through the door, it fell off, depositing Shane at the foot of the gate. The team erupted into huge cheers. A man walking his dog, stopped, looked suspiciously at the scene and then hurried off. Shane threw the door in the bushes and eventually managed to get Hogwarts to open up. After a long pristine drive with perfect rugby pitches on either side for what seemed miles, they arrived at the clubhouse, with Shane driving without a door. He told the team he was going to front it out. He said they wouldn't know if he drove without a door normally. It might throw them off a bit was his reasoning.

The clubhouse looked like it had never had dirty boots anywhere near it. As the team looked for the changing rooms, Ashley arrived with Serge. There weren't many people around the club at the time as this match was akin to training. When the Frenchman, walked past the few that were, they did a double take. In their minds they said 'that's Serge Sella' but then realised it was Badcock, so couldn't possibly be.

Ashley and Howley clapped the teams as they ran out. The Smitherwick guys looked as though they'd just hit puberty and bristled with fitness and verve. Serge came out last. Badcock didn't have a no 12 shirt to fit him, so they got a blank one from lost property and painted a white number badly on its back. It had run at the bottom like a horror movie effect. The home side supporters who hadn't seen Serge arrive, all nudged each other, shook their heads, one even cleaned his glasses. Suddenly there was a very angry coach in a tracksuit shouting as he ran towards Ashley and Howley. He eventually got in their faces.

"What the fuck's that?" he shouted.

"Well I'd hope you recognise a rugby pitch when you see one," the Welshman said with a smirk. This succeeded in winding the coach up even more, making him stutter as he tried to get his words out in rage.

"I'm talking about that fucking Frenchman running out in your kit."

"Oh Serge. Yes, he joined us the other day. He's quite a player you know," Ashley said really enjoying himself.

"This is illegal. You can't have a fucking international playing for you."

"Ex-international."

"I don't care if he's an ex sheep,"

"Well that doesn't work," Ashley said.

"Bit weird," Howley said.

"Listen you pair of wankers, you're not going to get away with this. I'll make sure of it,"

"There's nothing you can do," they said in unison.

"I'm phoning Mike right away and get this game cancelled."

"You can call who like boyo, it's all legit."

Ashley had called Michael Hunt as soon as Serge said yes. After some email exchanges, he got another from mikehunt@badsewage.com

Dear Ashley,

Thanks for all the paperwork re Mr Sella. I can confirm all is in order, and he is now registered to play in the Hunt Sewage Tournament from immediate effect.

On a personal note, I'd like to thank you for bringing Mr Sella to our county and tournament. I don't know how you managed it, but it is wonderful for our little tourney to have a player of such world-class involved.

I will not let the other teams know, they will find out as soon as he runs on the pitch for the first time. It's going to cause quite a stir, I can tell you. I'll have to set up a owners/mangers' hotline.

Please do let me know which match he will be his first, it would be honour to meet a true superstar of the world game. Wild horses won't stop me being there, and I do hope you can introduce us.

Kindest regards

Michael

Their coach stormed over to his players and told them to not play until he sorted it out. On cue, Michael got out of his Ranger in the car park and was immediately accosted by the incensed coach. Eventually, the shouting stopped, and the manager's shoulders slumped. He traipsed over to his players, ordered them back onto the pitch and trudged off to the sideline.

Serge didn't disappoint. The difference between an international, world-class, professional player and a grassroots even semi-pro player cannot be overstated. Of course, the physical attributes are the first thing to consider. Every muscle and tendon, has been worked on relentlessly to produce the perfect physique for a rugby player in their position. It wasn't just a matter of going down the gym and pumping some iron. It was a science, finely tuning every sinew used to provide optimal output for the outcome. When Sella stepped off his right foot, having received the ball, the unilateral exercises he had done on each muscle grouping in his legs, all worked in tandem. Everything was moulded for the best result, much like building a robot. Then there was the way his rugby brain worked. An awareness of space, of where everyone is on the pitch, seeing gaps he knew he could exploit, knowing what his opponents were going to do and how they would react to what he was doing. He played everyone like a conductor in front of his orchestra. He made all look as though they were kids playing an adult.

On top of all that, no-one could hardly get near him all game, including the Badcock players. When the opposition made contact in what they thought would be a tackle, the combination of his physical and mental skills, they just bounced off him. He scored eight tries, including two intercepts. Even to Ashley, he could see how special this player was and how, compared to any other team in the tournament, he was going to rip them to shreds. His presence and brilliance stirred Wilkinson and Faf into a hitherto unknown level. Truly world-class players do that, they bring people up in their level by just being there doing what they do. There were some lovely interplays between the three midfield players, something Howley couldn't believe he'd been watching. Sella even gave Faf a walk-in try as he once again broke through all the opposition defenders. Howley beamed, David and Breeda who'd made it along, were shouting their hearts out. Smitherwick scored a try but were humiliated by Town.

FT Smitherwick 10 Badcock Town 62

When the final whistle went, every one of their players ran over to Serge to shake his hand. Their no 12 asked to swap shirts, which the smiling Sella duly obliged with. Phones were brought on from, and many, many selfies were posed for. Delusionary dad approached them on the touchline.

"Finally a player to back my son up. Giving him the support he deserves, to let his talent shine through."

"It's what he needed all along," Ashley said, pleased with himself that he was making a sarcastic joke about a rugby player.

"Well, yes, I know. It's what I've been saying."

"You two should work out some plays this weekend at home so he can share them with the team next week in training," Howley had taken it to another level. The wheels were turning in Dad's mind, he could sense there was a some pisstake being had, but he really did believe in his son's ability. He sort of shuffled off unsure if he'd been the target of a joke.

One of the home team's dad was a sports reporter, he called the office.

"You're never gonna to believe who just played against my son in the Hunt Sewage tournament," he told the duty editor back in the office. The news went out online within minutes. A couple of drinks in the clubhouse (Ashley on water) led to a lot more snapping, signing and an intro to Mike. By the time Ashley was ready to take the Frenchman home, a fair crowd had gathered outside the clubhouse, all with their phones out and Smitherwick shirts offered for him to sign. He obliged them all with warmth and humility. Although he hated the stardom, he loved rugby and knew that any of the kids guys could be World Cup winners, so would never refuse someone an autograph or selfie. He was aware that it could stay with them all their lives. It did for him when he got the autograph of world player of the year at the time, an All Black, after they had thrashed France. That was when he knew what he wanted to do with his life.

"That was fun," Serge said to Ashley as they drove away. "Now we shall have some wine yes."

"Sorry, I'm under strict instructions to get you back to London safely."

They chatted about anything but rugby, which suited Ashley

fine. It turned out Ashley had been on holiday to Bayonne, where Serge was from. He got the low down on the finer points of dairy farming in the region and how it produced the best cheeses in France. It was all in the manure they use for the grass the cows grazed on. The waste from the finest pigs was mixed with the finest wheat and natural minerals from the region. It was fair to say Serge was a proud Basque man. Other topics were cheese or dessert first, what wine should you use in boeuf bourguignon and why French police sirens sound broken. Ashley loved it, the car journey flew by. It wasn't rugby, children, money or Hans.

17

Ashley met Fiona in *The Boot* in London's West End. It was a pub that dated back to medieval times. In those days, publicans would hang decorative items outside their public houses to distinguish themselves from the surrounding properties thus making it easier for customers to find and then stumble out of. This was a tradition still seen outside most pubs in the modern UK with a sign depicting a dancing pony or hairy goat. The current incarnation of *The Boot* would have had the first-ever landlord turning in their grave. It had stayed a spit and sawdust pub until a year previously when the business rent and rates got too high for selling pints to old geezers with tales of the gangsters of old. They just didn't have the spending power to support the publican. A famous restauranteur bought it for a steal off the landlord who just wanted shot of the whole business and retire. The new owners were a successful high-end restaurant group backed with hedge fund money. They owned and ran private clubs and eateries in London and New York. They wanted to keep the character of *The Boot* in its medieval roots

Now a private members' club but still a pub, just a very expensive one with nice food. Thais got them membership, and the first time Ashley was there, he ordered two gin and tonics. He was presented with a card machine showing £60 by the bar person. He was going to ask that there surely had been a mistake and that there were muggers who would demand less. But he didn't want to show himself up in front of London's cool people. He nonchalantly just tapped as if it were expected even though he wanted to grab the manager and ask how on god's green earth, they could charge that for a couple of G&TS. He was told later that the gin had been distilled on the Mongolian Steppes using juniper berries that grew at very rare springs that even the local shepherds didn't know about. The stills where this elixir of life fermented, were created in the ground using toothpicks fashioned from ancient, even magical, woodlands. When done, herders of wild horses transported the gin to a modern port. The containers were made from the stomachs of rare Yaks found only in one area. As it was his business, Ashley could spot company nonsense from a mile off. He envisaged the still was actually a rusty old petrol tanker out the back of the sheds at the port and that the berries were most likely the 'dingle' berries Australians call the bits of dung that stick to the wool around a sheep's bottom. The PR BS allowed the makers to charge a king's ransom for what was no different from normal gin. The drinks industry had been doing this sort of bushwacking for decades. All the so-called 'premium' vodkas, gins, and spirits that you needed a mortgage to drink, did not differ in taste warranted by the difference in price. The owners justified the stratospheric prices because of restoration, resulting in none of the old stuff being there, it was all reproduction.

When Ashley suggested the venue to Fiona, she seemed impressed and said that she'd wanted to try it for ages but didn't know any members. Ashley felt cool again, he'd impressed a girl for the first time in what seemed like a very long time. He thanked Thais internally for doing it for them. It had become a great investment, if not an eye-watering one. Ashley enjoyed seeing Fiona at the rugby club, especially as she wasn't Howley, Budgie or any of the boys. He'd taken to checking her rota so as to avoid her not being at the club when he was.

He was early, so a coke zero at the bar was the order of the day. There were two pretentiously loud guys beside him. Every time one would say something positive about somewhere in the world one simply had to visit, the other would try to outdo the location. They were easily the most insufferable bores Ashley had ever encountered. He wasn't a violent person but would have loved to have Budgie punch them.

She never made it to the Serge party as she was ill, so when she walked in, Ashley took a breath. He'd never seen her in civvies, out of workout gear, or in a social setting. What struck him immediately was her style. All in black, with a relaxed black trouser suit, white shirt untucked and box-fresh white trainers. Ashley didn't really know, but he guessed it was all very expensive. He realised he'd also never seen her hair out of a ponytail. She oozed class and inner confidence. This being the first time meeting out of work, Ashley was unsure how to greet her. Did he shake hands, do nothing and greet as he would in the clubhouse with a jaunty hi or did he go for the kiss? He ended up to doing a mixture of all three in a very awkward fashion. She dealt with his discomfort in a relaxed and at ease fashion. This just made Ashley more nervous. He started asking himself why was he nervous, what was he playing at?

"So what do you think?" he asked her once she'd sat down.

"It's nice, cool keeping all the old stuff."

"I had you pegged for the person who moved in these circles," Ashley said,

"What gave you that impression?"

"Well you know, the family, the ex," she seemed a bit riled by this question.

"Just because, my family have a bit of money and I have a few famous clients, doesn't make me any sort of person. They're just things." A slightly awkward silence ensued as Ashley tried to work out if this was going to be worse than pulling teeth or as fun as he'd envisaged.

"What do you reckon about our chances?" Fiona asked, changing the subject.

"Good, good. But let's not talk about the club, work and all that." Ashley hadn't invited her out to talk about the club. He wanted to know more about her.

"Ok, what shall we talk about?" she asked not uncomfortable with Ashley's direction. He didn't seem the type that, as a married man, he was going to hit on her in a creepsville way. If he did, she would have been able to handle it.

"What happened with the ex?" Ashley asked going right in.

"He cheated on me."

"Oh, sorry."

"With my best friend."

"Shit, no way. Sounds like a Jeremy Kyle episode," Ashley chortled and immediately regretted it when he saw Fiona's face.

"He hurt me to the core of my being. I thought he was the one. The one I would spend the rest of my life with, have children, build a family." Ashley was really regretting that joke. "He then ripped my heart out, and they both stamped on it until it was mush."

"Oh God. I'm so sorry. I didn't mean to be flippant. I always say stupid things at the wrong time." Ashley was used to having to apologise for something he said. He had joke Tourette's, i.e. if he thought something was funny, he would just blurt it out, not thinking about how it might go down. She stared at him motionless and then smiled warmly and reached for her drink.

"It's OK, how were you to know? I suppose it is a bit like that." More drinks were ordered. She wanted an Espresso Martini, a fine drink but usually not so early in an evening. They were normally the sign that the night was about to get a bit rowdy.

"Have you ever been cheated on Ashley?" Now it was his turn to be a bit taken aback by the directness of the conversation. Those martinis had started to kick in.

"Nope."

"Lucky man."

"Nor have I ever cheated on anyone."

"One in a million. A real catch."

"Would you mind telling my wife that." They smiled together.

"She's very beautiful."

"I know, out of my league right?"

"Why do you say that?"

"That's what people always say, it's true though. I'm all right with that."

"I don't think it is true. She's lucky to have you. Trust me." Ashley was having a conversation all to himself in his mind. She couldn't have been flirting with him could she? No, of course not. Ridiculous idea.

"Do you love her?"

"Well, er, er, yes."

"If it were me, I would have wanted more commitment for you."

"What do you mean?"

"Well, if someone asks someone if they love their partner, it should be a resounding yes straight away. No umming and ahhing, like you just did."

"We're working through a few things at the moment, but we'll get there."

The conversation continued for a fair few more drinks, although it was Fiona doing the actual drinking. They covered all the bases with plenty of laughter until she got emotional when talking about the situation that happened with Fortesque and her mum. She was angry at them both but spitting blood at him. He was the one who broke the family up, he was the one who chased her mum, then left her to her own devices when the affair was discovered. To her, he was a scurrilous shyster with the moral compass of an alley cat. It was clear to Ash how much Smythe had hurt her.

18

The excitement around Serge playing had gone international, which put Ashley in his element. There were interview requests from mainstream TV, Press, magazines, rugby influencers and every other Tom, Dick and Harry across the world. Everyone wanted a piece of what was a hero's story about a French superstar saving an English grassroots club. It didn't just encapsulate rugby's ethos and values, it was something to touch the soul, a feel-good story. Ashley had even been approached for the film rights, assuming they won and the club was saved. He and Serge came up with a plan to deal with the press. Sella would answer a whole list of questions just once (with Howley adding some words). The PR man would then distribute it as a press release, which could be quoted as though the interviewer was asking the questions directly. They couldn't use the word exclusive or imply it was. Because everyone was lazy, and that was all they were getting, the number of publications and so-called journalists that used the 'interview' was astounding.

IV: I can't believe I'm saying these names in the same sentence but why is Serge Sella playing for a team like Badcock Town?

SERGE: I'd had enough of the professional game in France, in fact the professional game overall. When I first got into rugby, I'd grown up on stories from my grandfather about the non-professional international teams. The forwards had faces that only their mothers would love. Halftime in the changing room was a beer and a cigarette. It was like a UFC fight in the rucks where if you didn't expect a shoeing, you were doing something wrong. The mercurial backs were nothing like the huge bristling units of the modern game. They were bandy-legged, skinny and had ridiculous hair with sideburns. They could swerve, dance, twist and turn in an instant. Once the rough stuff was done and they got the ball, they would tear teams apart like no one else. They all did it for the love of it, for the love of playing the game and playing the game with their mates. So when I got the opportunity to get back to that, at Badcock, I said yes.

IV: But you didn't have any of that old stuff. You came into the professional era and clubs?

SERGE: "Yes but I just grew upset at the way players were exploited around the world.

IV: Surely you miss running out in front of 80,000 fans?

SERGE: Of course. It is the greatest honour in my life to play for France, especially at home. Mon Dieu, to win the World Cup, I mean, what kid who loves rugby hasn't dreamt of winning the World Cup.

IV: Then why give that up?

SERGE: The structure had just become sterile, the love for the game, for me, had gone.

IV: You're this superstar who plays–played–at the highest level. How can you run out with those guys and care?

SERGE: This is rugby. They are my teammates now.

IV: But most of them aren't even good enough to clean your boots, let alone belong on the same pitch as you?

SERGE: We are in it together, no egos. It doesn't matter what level we're playing at. We all want to get through each match in this tournament without losing, then celebrate together afterwards. We all want to win the final so we are all bound by the same goal. To me, that makes us all on the same level as people and as rugby players.

IV: The match game plan must surely just give you the ball. Job done?

SERGE: No. Even the most junior of sides can tackle. And actually, I've found so far, everyone puts in an extra bit of effort in the tackle. They are as ferocious as any international I've played in. *He was being gracious. In the one game he'd played so far, the tacklers did try and put a bit more into it, but they were swatting* *a fly with a postage stamp.* So we need each player to do their job, win set pieces, exit, kick/chase. It's an old cliché, but do the basics first and always first, then see what happens.

IV: So what else have you found strange here?

SERGE: I don't get that brown water you drink. Bitter I think it's called. Why? What purpose does that have when it comes to taste? I just don't know.

IV: Badcock Town, the place not the rugby club, it's not Bayonne, how have you adapted?

SERGE: I'm staying in London *(note to editors–insert 'He gave a Gallic shrug and warm smile' where you feel necessary.)*

IV: How have your teammates taken to playing with a Six Nations and World Cup-winning superstar?

SERGE: They haven't changed at all, everyone, including me, still has to get to the toilet before Budgie.

IV: What's the reaction back in France, what about your fellow internationals?

SERGE: They think I'm mad and some of them have been going on about how crazy I am on socials, etc.. But my real friends know how important rugby is to my life. Not the slick product that the professional game is, but the rugby played in the mud, with friends, family and supporters making the matches a social occasion where you share a glass of wine and some cheese. You know we have the finest cheese in all of France, it's to do with the manure.

IV: What about the food, the English are famous in France for terrible food.

SERGE: That is so wrong, the restaurants I've been to here are just as good as the ones in France. There are some dishes I really think are terrible though.

IV: Like what?

SERGE: My teammates gave me a deep-fried mars bar and said it was a delicacy here, prized as the best you can get in England. I nearly threw up when I ate it.

IV: That's a Scottish thing. So are you guys going to win to the tournament and save the club?

SERGE: Oi.
IV: What will you do when that's done
SERGE: My cows need me.

Game 5 back at home. If they progressed, BTRFC would always have a home tie, Shane had seen to it. Tradition dictated that the important role of pulling bits of paper out of a bucket was the Financial Director at Hunt. Shane had a bit on him (something to do with a sexual practice known as tarmaccing) so asked him to make sure that Badcock always got drawn first, which got home advantage. He also tried to dictate which team they would face, but the way the draw was conducted didn't allow for such shenanigans.

When Ashley arrived in the car park, he couldn't find a spot near the clubhouse. This irritated him, there was always room there, but not this time. Even though it was a cold day, there were a crowd of people standing around outside the clubhouse drinking their pints out of plastic cups. Many of them had cameras slung around their necks or held microphones with wires leading into their pockets. He could spot a journo at 100 yards and there was a gaggle of them–at his club. He didn't recognise any of them as they were sports journos, not his normal MO. He was minded to tell them not to display all their kit out in the open wastelands of Badcock if they wanted to keep it, but then thought 'tough'. David and Breeda were doing the honours at the beer tables. They decided to keep them outside even though it was a bit nippy as they thought it was good luck.

"What's going on, why haven't I got my normal space?"

"Jaysus, don't they know who you are?" Ashley made a mental note to make sure he had a space with a sign and his name so no one could take it again.

"Never seen anything like this here, I don't think we've got insurance for more than 30 people," David said.

"This number of people in this area, usually means they're rioting," Breeda said.

Supporters had arrived from both clubs, including ones from

Badcock that had never been to the club before. The cars were parked all the way down the lane leaving little space for Mini, let alone all the SUVs not normally associated with the Badcock. There was definitely more wax jackets than tracksuits although the home supporters stood out as if Wally wore a flashing green and ink top instead of a red striped one. The assortment of neck tattoos, knock-off gear and the cheapest cigarettes they could get off the back of the lorry signposted them.

Ashley started walking to join Howley who was watching a warm up marshalled by Fiona. This was another new facet to the club's games. They'd seen them on the tele but a warm-up had possibly involved a pint and a fag before. They were reluctant at first as to the point of a warm up. She had to explain the science behind ensuring a muscle is warm and in use before it was immediately exposed to high intensity pressure. One player came up with a cock joke but was soon reduced to a little Chihuahua by the stare of Fiona. That was the last time lads' humour was attempted. Whilst England weren't going to worry about the injury status of Budgie, nor were the Boks hounding Howley to make sure Faf didn't pull a hamstring, Howley wanted to embrace the philosophy wholeheartedly. What he wanted, the players did. Delusional dad approached, but Ashley couldn't turn away or hide.

"Why isn't my son playing?"

"You need to ask Howley that I'm afraid."

"Same old story, his talent ignored. Fucking club, you're just as bad as the last tosser," he said angrily, shuffling off. Ashley finally made it to Howley.

"I've just seen our favourite dad, why isn't Dusty playing?"

"Because he's shit."

"Hasn't he always been shit?"

"You started this boyo. We now have a tournament to win. With Sella, we can, so if I can find anyone from our cesspit pool of players to help him, and us, do this, I will.

"Who took his place?"

"You don't know him, he's Grave Robber's son." Ashley had

given up on asking why people were called various nicknames. He realised that he would meet whoever was being referenced and it would become apparent like someone called tiny who was a giant. He later found out that grave robber was literally that, he used to dig up graves of rich people for any loot they were buried with. He mistakenly believed they took the booty with them.

Serge hadn't trained with the team, but you didn't need to when you were a world-class centre playing grassroots rugby. During the week, Howley worked with the team on various plays, but they all involved one thing–getting the ball to Serge. Howley told the mercurial Frenchman his playbook but Serge was unhappy that he'd become the focus of the way they were going to play.

"Listen boyo, I know you're only here for the tourney, and then you're off. For now, you are our Superman, no cape, more a cockerel. You could save this club from bankruptcy. The boys are relying on you to make sure they've got this place to play for next season. You know what it's like to belong, to play for each other, to hit, bleed and hurt for each other. So now, do me a favour and make sure you kick every arse that's out in front of you."

Howley had identified Serge's soul, the reason why he played and the reason why he came to Badcock.

FT Badcock Town 48 Deep Bottom 7

Sella did the business again.

19

Ashley's local, the *Prickly Bush,* was nestled at the bottom of a mansion block near Victoria Station. It had been around since Moses, festooned with worn swirly carpet, a dart board, horseshoes nailed to the fake wooden beams and all the sports channels on the two corner TVs. Old notes from around the world were pinned to every inch of the back wall. Those international travellers who stumbled in thinking it was one of those famous English pubs, ended up giving over a note to the landlord almost at gunpoint.

This was not Ashley's normal habitat, but like the many souls in there, it was an escape. They were escaping from loneliness, their partner or just from a sad life where they had nothing else to do. In Ashley's case, it was an oasis get away from home for a moment. Many evenings when walking the dog, he popped in, bought a Coke Zero, got a bowl for the dog and sat at the bar. He observed the various regulars in their habitat, like a public house naturalist. Being on first-name terms with them all in no way meant were they his friends. He never met anyone outside the confines of the Bush and definitely never had any of them around to his house. Ashley didn't have any of their numbers saved in his phone bar one guy 'hairy bush' who was a very hairy drunk stranger in there once. Ashley would normally make various comments on discussions going on around him but only when asked and kept it at that, he didn't want to get involved in a conversation he'd never get out of. Of course, Thais didn't normally allow him to frequent the pub, especially such a terrible one, but she couldn't be bothered to walk the dog walk so allowed him that sin.

"Dog thirsty then Bob," said Derek, wearing his usual leather waistcoat and faded Van Halen t-shirt. Sporting a face like a wet flannel and greasy long and thinning hair. He always span a yarn about girls he went out with, to the belief of absolutely no one. The only girls he met were on Pornhub.

"Yep," Ashley had given up telling him it wasn't Bob.

"You know, the average dog has the ability to learn words like a two-year-old kid."

He'd arranged to meet Howley here after finding out he was in town. Ashley could have gone to *The Boot* but didn't want to look like he was showing off. He thought his local would be more Howley's type of place. Ashley expected him to look around as if all was new when he walked in.

"Howley!" shouted Derek. When he sat down with a couple of pints

"How does Derek know you?"

"Victoria is the train station I come into whenever I'm up."

"I've never seen you in here."

"Derek was a regular in the one I do go to round the other side. I think he got banned from there solely because the landlord got bored of his endless shite." Shared ground already, maybe this would be as bad as Ashley imagined.

"So how are the boys?" Howley smirked in appreciation.

"Good."

"So far, we've done ok right?"

"That we have."

"You must have wondered what I was about when I first rocked up there?"

"I thought you were a complete cock."

"I'm hoping there's a but there." Howley paused and looked at Ashley without emotion.

"You might have turned out OK."

"Don't go too far overboard, people will think you're going soft."

Howley returned from the bar with a couple of pints. Ashley was taking a break from no alcoholic beverages. They got talking about Howley's days as a player. The Welshman told the story of how it ended for him. It was the Five Nations, Italy only made it the Six Nations in 2000. Scotland v Wales at the Murrayfield. The whole team was bussed to a spot an hour outside Edinburgh, which was supposed to replicate a highland environment. They would all drink, bond and feel the spirit of kilted ones who were going to come at them with all their might. The game was the championship decider for the Scottish so the Welsh wanted to get the feeling of where the team they were facing, came from.

The bus broke down at its destination. This was the time of no mobiles and no internet. They were on their own, no one would know they were missing until they didn't turn up for the breakfast in the hotel the morning of the match. So the transport stranded in the countryside with just beer as an emergency kit, there was nothing for it but try and push the bus back. They were rugby players after all so were used to rucking. As they were pushing, Howley's foot went down a rabbit hole resulting in a broken ankle at a nasty position that meant it never healed properly. He played one more game for Wales two years later but it wasn't the same. He couldn't run or put any strain on it in the way he used to be able to. With all the young fellas coming up the ranks, he slipped out of the coaches' eyes and never got picked again. Welsh career over.

Another pint later, Davies opened up.

"For the past 20 years or so, I haven't known a time when I woke up, looked in the mirror, and said–hey, you're good laddie. I only hung on at the club because Jockey made me. If it wasn't for him, I'd probably be in a gutter somewhere with no teeth, drinking meths."

"Jesus Howley, I didn't realise it was so bad. I mean you look like shit, so I could guess things weren't great but could never have guessed your mental state had gone that far." The pints were starting to do their self-editing trick on him.

"A bit of advice boyo, counselling as a career, it's not for you"

"Sorry, I just spit out stuff without thinking. What about your brother? You're in the same county for fuck's sake!"

"We were never that close, even before our little incident."

"Look, I want to help. You and I may have had our differences, but I never want to see a fellow human being, even one as cantankerous as you, suffer"

"You have done that, this tourney has made me realise why I loved rugby in the first place. Sella has brought back my enthusiasm for the game, the boys, the camaraderie, and belonging. It's what this club, this game has given me in the past and will do so for a long time, assuming we don't go bust of course."

"Well with our French help, we may well survive, and then onwards right." Of course, Ashley couldn't tell Howley about the future plans to concrete the club over, but that could wait for another time. More pints were fetched.

"You obviously don't know Breeda's surname, or else you will have made a crap joke about it."

"I take exception to that insinuation. You're right though, I don't."

"Rabett!"

"Rabbit? Breed a rabbit?"

"It's pronounced ra-bett in Ireland."

"We're not in Ireland."

"Don't ever mention it to her, the last guy who made a joke about it was never seen again. They think he was fed to Tyson"

"Who's that?"

"Shane's dog."

"Of course it is. So the sarciest person I've ever met, who'd take the piss out Mother Theresa, is called Breeda Rabbitt." Ashley was laughing so hard, tears were appearing in his eyes, Howley couldn't help but join in too, just without the tears.

20

Ashley sat at the breakfast bar in his kitchen and read the Sundays' sport pages, something he never used to do before. There were numerous 'funnies', stories where the headline posed a question like 'Guess where French superstar is playing his rugby right now?' One writer suggested it could be a popular pub quiz question 'What team beginning with B did World Cup winner Serge Sella play for in the UK?' Josh called from Singapore.

"It's fair to say your boy's caused a bit of a stir in the rugby world."

"What even out there?"

"We do have the internet you know."

"I owe you man. He could be our saviour. We can definitely win this crappy little tournament with him."

"If he stays there right."

"He's pledged to me he will see it out all the way. He enjoyed the last game, a few more and he can go back to his cows."

"You see, you didn't need me then."

"Oh I did."

Thais came into the kitchen holding a scrum cap. She hung out from her hip like a flag.

"What this?"

"It's called a scrum cap and is there to protect the head."

"And why it here?"

"It's Harry's." He had normally gone with Thais on matters of bringing up the kids, but he was starting to get a feeling the other way on this one. Yes, it was dangerous, but so was crossing the road. If properly supervised and protected, he saw no reason to stop them from doing something they wanted to do. There had been many sad stories of ex-players with conditions caused by taking bangs to the head. But the protocols and equipment that existed in the modern game, were there to protect players and mitigate such outcomes. It was exercise, taught you about teamwork, playing for your mates and was fun. Of course, unlike cricket which was always played in summer, its home was in autumn/winter, in the mud, cold and rain. That was part of the fun for the kids so Ashley wasn't going to argue with them.

"We speak about this, they not play it."

"You tell them then." He'd hit on the motherload with this one. It was rarely used by any partner because it needed impact to be effective. Brought into play too much, and the power goes making it is as useful as a chocolate teapot. The 'Well I think they're ok. They're having fun, they love doing it. Are you going to be the one to ruin that for them?' card. She took a huge deep breath, looked at him and realised she'd been bested - for now. It wasn't worth the nuclear tears and huffs, yet. As she stomped off, Ashley felt somewhat pleased with himself. The phone rang again.

"Ashley Havers?" asked the voice.

"Yes."

"My name's Jude Sexton, and I'm a journalist with All About Rugby." Ashley knew him well. In fact, everyone in PR knew him well. He'd been a big political writer (books, TV appearances, lectures and the rest) for a decade or so. In that time, many stories surfaced in the industry about his sexual proclivities. His supposed exploits would have put any MP to shame. The sexual appetite knew no bounds and he got the reputation for the guy 'who'd do a cracked plate.' There was an internal investigation at the paper that employed him when a picture emerged of him carrying out a sexual act on a sex toy whilst doing a line of coke with a prostitute. She was the one who took the photo and sold the story. He became a pariah in the industry. This call from 'Jude sextoy' was particularly satisfying for Ashley. As a young PR, his client was an ambitious MP who had eyes on making a name for himself. Havers was engaged to get good stories out there about the public servant. The usual fare - secret charity work, putting up refugees, helping out at food banks, etc. Ashley pitched a story to Jude and a couple other of his colleagues. Sexton dressed him down in front of the meeting and belittled his skills and work. Then he disappeared into a backroom with a young intern. After the scandal broke, he disappeared off the radar for a few years, only to emerge into the sporting journalist world.

"I remember you Jude, how can I help you?" Sexton clearly didn't remember Ashley.

"Well, I'm doing a story on your boy Serge. Quite a coup I have to say."

"Yes, it was."

"It's just that when I contacted his people, they told me to talk to you. Is that right?"

"Yes."

"Ok, so how do I get to interview him?"

"I'll send you an interview all the press can use."

"I'm not some wankstain intern you know. I want to talk to him myself."

"I'm afraid that won't be possible."

"Listen shithead, I don't know what experience you have in dealing with the press, but I'm a respected journalist and this guy is fucking rugby superstar. You're messing with the big boys you fucking cockwomble."

"Goodbye Mr sextoy."

It was a busy morning on the blower. Smythe was next.

"Putting a little run together there chief."

"Ah, I was wondering when I'd hear from the landed gentry." Ashley had grown into this whole thing. He was enjoying the collective goal, he even found sparring with various types enjoyable.

"You've been lucky so far but I'm telling you, you won't get away with Brie boy for the next match."

"I don't like your racism Fortesque."

"I will not let you do this. I will have that fucking club. You and your band of merry fuckheads won't be able to stop it."

"I'm sure you feel that's the case Smythe, you may find events will turn out differently."

"You jumped up little shit. Get given an awful club that you hate, and now think you're Eddie Jones."

"It's growing on me," Thais came in.

"Who that?"

"That fat prick Fortesque."

"That club change you, to worse. I want you out bad place, my kids out danger game, and all move on."

Geoff the dopey bulldog ambled over and collapsed his head at Ashley's feet. He broke wind. He'd been prone to this recently and Budgie would have been proud. The dog was so old, they couldn't remonstrate with him. They tried it and he just raised his head in a way as if to say 'Enough of the histrionics guys. You don't get to my age to hold those things in. So tough, get used to them.'

There was one other media outlet that was agreed Sella would talk to, the main British broadcaster for the English Premiership. They'd built up a reputation for excellent coverage with innovations, a wealth of ex-internationals and unrivalled coverage of most games.

Ashley had been approached by them. The email said:

Dear Mr Havers,

With the whole rugby world interested in such a wonderful story, we want to broadcast your remaining games in the tournament (the semi and the final) live on our network. Perhaps you could give my assistant a call to arrange coming in to discuss this.

Yours sincerely,

Hugh Jarse.

Director of Broadcast.

When Ashley forwarded it on to Howley, he just replied 'Holy

Fuck.' The author of the email's title was the expectation for the meeting but when Havers turned up at reception, he was told it would be taken by Agate Blanco, the chairperson of the whole shooting match. Whilst waiting in reception, he Googled her and immediately became nervous. First, she happened to be French and a properly huge fan of Monsieur Sella, as everyone seemed to be. Second, she had a formidable reputation of being more hard-ass than any other TV executive in the business. She was known as the Agaterminator. Starting as a junior reporter, she blasted her way up the ranks in sport TV with an uncanny nose for a story. She had no fear and no inhibitions about being in a male-dominated industry. She was just better than all her male counterparts. She rose to MD of one of the main channels in the network stable within a few years. Having developed the skill of deal maker extraordinaire, the boardroom became littered with the corpses of powerful club owners and other TV execs far more experienced than her. Five years later, she became chairperson of the entire network, still with the fierce appetite for a deal and a story. She'd been a long time rugby fan. Ever since she saw the phenomena, Jonah Lomu, run over England players for fun at the 1995 RWC. She loved the sheer brutality of that performance by the NZ great. Yes they were the broadcaster of choice for the professional game, but for her, this man playing at BTRFC to help save them from going broke was a win win everywhere she looked. They'd be able to get subscriptions by the hundreds of thousands just because of Sella. The rugby wouldn't be great, but the viewers wouldn't be watching for that. It was a fairy-tale battle of the grassroots underdogs against the big bad world with Serge as the superstar hero saving the day. There was also the element that Ashley wasn't going to be the calibre of owners she usually clashed heads with. She banked on getting this for a song.

"Quite a thing you've going on down there in?" Agate said as she paused and gestured to Ashley to help her out. All part of the negotiating quick step.

"Badcock Town," he helped out.

"Ah yes, that's the one. So we want to do something you will never have ever been involved in before and broadcast a couple of live games from your club."

"Yes," Ashley said confidently. He'd rehearsed this a fair few times and the gull incident wasn't going to throw him off track. "That's great, how much are you going to pay?"

"Are you a rugby man, Mr Havers?"

"I'm finding my feet."

"Well then, you surely know that we only ever broadcast the crème de la crème of the sport?"

"I'm aware."

"So why would we be interested in a shitty little club and tournament like yours?"

"Oh I don't know, David and Goliath? Heroes coming from the ashes and saving their club?"

"Oh yes, of course that's it. Thank you Mr Havers for putting me straight, I'd been looking at it from the wrong angle altogether."

"I'll level with you." His strategy was to fess up, no point trying to play big boy games. He wanted money to survive and that was the most important thing. "We need 200 k to stay afloat." He added a tad on. "So we'll take 300 for the two games plus exclusive access to the team." Although his first salvo was half of what she was prepared to pay, there was no way she was just going to give in that easy.

"I wouldn't pay a pound for access to that crappy team."

"Well. It's al part of the story, isn't it?."

"The story is not some bunch of criminals and misfits from a shitty town who can't play rugby," she said staring intensely at him without flinching a muscle.

"That's er, very unfair." Ashley got ruffled by the Superman stare coming from the other side of the desk. Silence. He shuffled in his seat, her face stayed focussed. It was his move. She'd happily wait an hour until he made it, just staring at him.

"Ah well, that does include Serge of course."

"Of course." She took a huge breath, still keeping up the eye contact. "We'll give you a hundred." Ashley tried to act that he was mulling such an insulting offer in his mind. He made faces hoping to impress upon her that it was a real dilemma. It wasn't. She just stayed like a brick with eyes – eyes on him.

"Well that's not enough."

"So is zero." He knew there was no point in carrying on playing negotiator.

"OK."

"Thought so. But there's one main condition. No Sella, no money."

"I'm sure that won't be a problem."

"I'm not having one of the biggest stars in world rugby disappear on me. Even though the money is pocket change for us, it goes against my sensibilities to pay for something and not get the thing I paid for. If I pay you for a penny chew, I expect and demand a penny chew. If I don't get a penny chew, I will ruin you to get the penny back."

"Don't worry, I can assure you, he's committed to us for the tournament."

21

Ashley was feeling chipper the morning of the semi-final. Driving through the entrance, sheriff had put a new sign on the gate. Shock horror, it looked professional and not like Stevie Wonder had put it up. It even had a light beneath it to illuminate in the dark Autumn afternoons. It was very early, but he could see that already cars were parking along the lane. He felt something he hadn't done before at the club–a sense of pride.

He'd secured a TV deal that meant they didn't need to win the tournament to stay alive. Get that semi match won and play a final. Done and dusted. Broadcaster fee in the bank, club safe, everyone happy. Yes, he was going to sell it eventually but he'd make sure all were looked after and had been talking to other local clubs about taking the membership and staff from BTRFC on board. All at the club were confident they'd win the whole tourney because they had Serge, their very own superhero who no other team in the tournament could live with.

As he reached the car park, something seemed to be missing. He couldn't put his finger on it straight away. Getting out of the car, he realised Shane's motorhome had gone. Miracle of miracles. It hadn't looked a good bet before. Ashley had to explain to the producer that moving the vehicle may be tricky. She needed it out of the way because cabling was needed from various bits of equipment like cameras around the pitch, to the trucks. She told Ashley to leave it to her, he doubted she'd get a result. TV riggers set up every bit of structure needed to get a broadcast out from the ground and 'rigged' all the cables, i.e. laid and plugged them in. They were used to dealing with all sorts, and there was always a way round a problem. One of them, Mickey, aka Metal Mickey, had the answer. He was a walking piercing advert–nose, ears, lips, skin on the inside of his mouth, nipples, penis, the skin in between his toes / fingers. He would have had his testicles done if it wasn't pointed out to him that he would either end up Bruce Jenner, hospitalised or dead. The firm he worked for couldn't ever send him abroad, unless on a ferry, as the time it took to get him through security meant he missed flights nearly every time. He had spotted Shane's penchant for S&M and invited him to a party that was the equivalent Met Galal if you liked that sort of thing. Shane was out of the car park before the rigger could even say BDSM.

There was a general buzz about the place that had never been experienced before. As well as what was missing, there was a number of rather large additions with the television outside broadcast trucks, cables everywhere, and people in headsets with 'crew' on the backs of their t-shirts rushing about, looking very busy. More cars than the club had ever known were parked, and this was early so more were to come. Supporters of both clubs were drinking and picnicking out the back of various 4 x 4s.

David and Breeda had set up the proper beer tent to the left of the clubhouse. They didn't actually do it themselves, Shane's mates in the marquee business did all that. It was almost the size of the clubhouse. Splendid in white with walls and even toilet areas at the back. A proper bar stood in the middle of the room with professionally arranged beer taps and wine bottles. Ashley shuddered a bit when he looked at all the barrels behind it. Shane had got them for a 'killer price', and he didn't want to think what lorry they'd fallen off. He just hoped they couldn't be traced back to the club. Rows of plastic glasses were stacked everywhere. The nations' flags had been relocated to the marquee, with the French one taking centre stage hanging off the front of the bar. A new flag for the club was hanging from the central spine of the roof, French again but huge and with a grinning Serge, in his international kit, showing off those famous pearly whites in the middle of it. Above his picture, BTRFC was crudely painted in black. Below his visage was 'Allez' as it was intended when the flag was manufactured but instead of the word 'France' following it, they had sellotaped a bit of white paper with 'Smurfs' painted on. The club had a hero they could get behind playing rugby rather than support when they came out of prison as usually happened. There was even a new electronic scoreboard donated by a local electrician who normally rented it out to one of the county's other sides.

Ashley watched as the camera crew set up an interview with Mike Hunt, who wanted to be at every game Sella played in. The sewage man had discovered a slight level of fame in the county on account of county media including local TV news. Once that seeped into a person's psyche, it's hard to get rid of. He'd walk down the high street and people would shout hello. People inherently want to be liked and needed, having someone shove a camera in your face and a reporter asking questions, is a drug.

The broadcaster had sent an anchor to Badcock. Normally, the main presenter had been a staple of their coverage. He had a cheeky chappy demeanour who messed about on camera with guests and pundits creating a 'ah he's here in the living room with us' feel. He not only loved his rugby, he knew it inside out. But he was doing the top-of-the-table clash on the main channel. So the presenter for Badcock Town RFC v Thyme-in-Thames RFC was Lydia Harrison. She was the captain and world cup winner with the England women senior team. She had become the poster child of the women's game with lucrative commercial contracts for advertising, writing and presenting. Viewers had particularly taken to her ability to be relaxed effortlessly on screen with pundits and players. Underlying this bonhomie was a serious analytical brain, an encyclopaedic knowledge of rugby in all its forms and serious respect from all players and ex-players. She stood with Mike in front of the camera on the touchline on a 22 by huge PA speaker that had magically appeared.. Ashley stood with the director behind.

"How did you react to the news of Sella's application to play here?" asked Harrison as she looked around and made a face as if to say 'This shithole' instead of 'here'.

"Well Lydia..." he got two words out before the tannoy kicked in. Ashley jumped at the sudden noise of Ritchie shouting greetings to everyone over the PA system.

"Cut!" shouted the director beside Ashley. They looked at each other as the shouting continued.

"Can you shut him the fuck up please?" the director asked. Ashley hurried off to find out how a PA system that he never knew existed, suddenly had burst into life. He hadn't noticed earlier that Ritchie had set up his DJ booth beside the outdoor bar. Resplendent in another truly horrific Hawaiian shirt under a coat, and freshly bleached side hair, the social secretary was on the mic.

"Come on the cocks!" he shouted but paused as soon as the owner loomed in his face. He looked up like a dog seeing his owner has the lead out for a walk.

"Keep it schtum Ritchie."

"What's that?"

"Shut the fuck up."

"Why?"

"I don't know if you've noticed but we've got the tele here. Your shouting on a PA system I never knew we had, is stopping us do interviews." Ashley said pointing over to the crew who were all looking back at them with faces of thunder. Woody had set up the speaker system the day before with two huge speakers positioned at each 22 on the clubhouse side of the pitch. No one had tested it for levels, so it was stuck on a level so high that the speakers shook when anything came out of them.

"Just trying to get some atmos going man," he said despondently.

"You can do that, just later. For now let us do the interviews." Like a petulant teenager, Ritchie went to hit the power button. When he touched it, he got an electric shock that knocked him backwards to the ground. Both speaker stacks did a good impression of an atomic bomb as they blew in an ear-splitting boom that made everyone instinctively duck.

"Feck'n woody strikes again,' Breeda said.

22

The players arrived one by one, early and looking like they owned the place. They had been given a swagger, one with a Gallic flavour, one that made them proud to get out of the cars, look around at the club and feel a sense of belonging and pride in what they were doing. Yes it was shitty Badcock, yes they had been shocking and couldn't beat an egg before. But now they were on the verge of the shit tournament final, plus they had moules. He was therein named that after one of the boys had questioned Serge about his favourite food. As well as the earthy stuff that farmers liked, he loved moules mariniere avec frites. The ones served on the coast near his farm were of course, the best in France. Something strange happened too.

"You fucking ready for this Bertie!" Faf shouted at Ashley as he passed him. The players had moved from openly mocking him totally dismissively to making him part of the humour. It was a subtle difference but one that tugged at Ashley's heart.

"Why call you Bertie?" Thais asked scathingly.

"Just part of the bants."

"What pants?"

"Don't worry about it," he said, smiling with an inner warmth she wouldn't understand. Ashley's phone went, it was Serge.

"Allo Ashley."

"Hi Serge, great atmosphere already, you on your way in?"

"I'm afraid not." Ashley suddenly got an ever so slight pain in his stomach.

"Oh?"

"I'm at the airport." That pain in his stomach turned into a twisting knife. "I'm so sorry Ashley but I have to go back to France, my flight boards in half an hour."

"Did you just say go back to France?"

"I can't tell you how sorry I am Ashley, but I must go back." His father had been out in the fields looking after the cows when he collapsed. Luckily a neighbour had been in the one opposite and called the ambulance. The dad was in hospital and they were unsure about his prognosis. He simply had to go back. There wasn't anything Ashley could say to Serge by way of admonishment. He wanted to scream though.

"Oh god, I hope he's ok."

"He's tough Ashley, he'll be ok, I hope too."

"I understand Serge, family always comes first."

"I've let you, Howley, Fiona and the boys down. I hope they will forgive me?"

"That won't be an issue. We will all be thinking of you and I know they'll play for you and your family."

"I will send them a message in the group."

"Best of luck Serge, I'll let you know how the game goes. I truly hope your father is ok and gets better quickly. Keep us updated."

"I will and thank you for being understanding." The call ended and Ashley looked up at the people busying themselves around the ground. Breeda was being interviewed,

"I'd have his fuck'n babies in a heartbeat."

"Cut," came the director's shout.

"Oh shite, I swore, sorry." They moved on just killing time until they got the one they were under orders 'not to fuck up'.

Ashley's stomach knot tightened, turned upside down and made him feel nauseous. The world was spinning as though he'd had a few beers. The club was sorted provided they played the semi and the final with Serge. They didn't need to win it to get the cash. He had left sale plans for the future to Thais, but he'd grown fond of the place and the people. He would deal with that issue after the club survived. He'd done a good job. Now that was all about to crash and burn like the Hindenburg. It wasn't just that they'd lose the TV money, but they also lost any chance of them winning the tourney with the Frenchman on the plane home. It would be Fortesque's after all. Fiona bounded up to him all full of beans.

"What's wrong, you look like you've seen a ghost?" she asked.

"Worse than that."

Fiona left Ashley to break it to the coach who he waited for in the clubhouse.

"Hey hey boyo," he shouted, he was unsurprisingly full of the joys of spring.

"I've got some bad news Howley."

"They haven't revoked your badminton society membership have they?"

"It's Serge." Davies sat down with a slightly concerned look on his face.

"Don't tell me, he's injured," he joked.

"Not injured, on his way back home." The cogs in Howley's brain were visible as he tried to process what had just been said.

"Home as in London hotel?"

"Home as in the pastures of South West France."

"Oh fuck!"

The coach waited until the team had gathered in the changing room. The guys, to a man, were silent and shocked, staring into the space in front of them.

"He had to do it boys. It's his family." Howley spoke in a measured Burtonesque manner. "Listen boys, remember what he fucking said right. We play for each other, we play for our mates, the lad going into every tackle every ruck, with your mates." He was starting to get through to them and a few nodded and shouted 'yes' "You understand! He's in France but what he taught us about this club and ourselves will fucking live on in all of us." More nods and shouts. "We'll play for him, and his dad right. We'll fucking play for each other." It was rousing them all.

"But all our plays are designed around Sella," Robinson burst the mood bubble.

"Look, I know these guys. They had someone at the last game watching us, making notes. They will have prepped and set their gameplan to deal with Sella."

"Like us," Robinson said.

"So, what we need to do," Howley continued, ignoring the full-back. "Is the exact fucking opposite of every play we'd have done with him. We need to surprise them, do unexpected things, different directions." He ran through some examples. "So on the Douglas Bader, instead of shifting it to the right, chuck it high over the ruck to the blind side. They will have loaded the openside to deal with Serge, so we have space there." It seemed like a good plan, but no-one was really convinced it would work.

Next up to tell were the producers. They had texted Ashley with a time for the pre-match and post-match interviews.

"I'm afraid Serge isn't playing today," he told the producer.

"Well that's our programme fucked then."

"He had to go back home because for family reasons."

"Welcome to the worst-rated programme on our whole network, ever."

"The story's still the same, little club trying to survive."

"I can't tell you the size of the shit, viewers don't give about your players, your games and this crap tournament."

"Shit tournament," Ashley surmised.

"Both are correct. This won't go down well with HQ," the producer said. When they parted, she dialled her phone. It wasn't long until Ashley's phone was ringing. The name flashing up on screen was Agate Blanco who he'd proudly saved with the title Chairperson. When it was entered in, he felt a frisson of excitement that a serious contact number gives. His black book was going to expand, and he'd be one of those people who would say, 'I'll introduce you to so and so.'

"What the fuck is going on? Why isn't Sella playing?" was her greeting.

"Understandable family reasons."

"Remember what I said about penny chews. Well, you haven't even given me one of those. Fuck your money Mr Havers, you won't get a single bit of it. In fact, I may sue you."

"It's hardly my fault."

"It's going to cost me a fucking king's ransom because of all the resources already in place. But fuck it! I'm pulling them out and the broadcast is off. Now that cost is what I will sue you for Mr Havers. See you in court."

Ashley didn't announce anything to the gathered supporters, he left that to David, who thanked him profusely for the task. They all were left disgruntled and cursing the 'cocks'. Free beer once again had to be doled out to quell any riotous behaviour.

TIT RFC were surprised when they didn't see Sella running out with the team. Their play book and approach to the game had disappeared down the toilet. It was designed on getting Serge, but now there was no mercurial Frenchman. Although far better players than Badcock, being thrown like that really affected their game. They made uncharacteristic mistakes the whole match. Forward passes, touch kicks out on the full, missing high balls.

FT Badcock Town 13 Thyme-in-Thames 12

Badcock won by a single point when Wilkinson kicked a penalty, the last kick of the game. Pandemonium ensued. Thais had to take the children back home, so she left Ashley to celebrate with the team. That was something he did with gusto, unfortunately for him.

23

He woke with a start and immediately felt a number of sensations. First was sheer alarm. He didn't recognise where he was, it was pitch black. Next came the pain like he'd been shot in the middle of his forehead. Then the inability to use his tongue. It'd been fused with the inside of his mouth after being glued with wallpaper paste. Thais had installed complete blackout curtains in the bedroom which always caused him problems on any given night. Their handmade oak bed looked fantastic and stylish but had one major flaw. With all their design experience, it seemed the makers couldn't design a bed that didn't have corners that were WMD. He smashed a shin nearly every night as he got up for a pee but didn't want to wake Thais up by turning the light on. He stumbled for his phone to throw some light on the matter, but it wasn't in any of his pockets.

He knew he was horizontal and stared upwards unable to move or decide what to do. Then another searing pain as everything went completely white. Thais had turned on the spotlights right above his head. The shock reaction of trying to turn away from the blinding light, caused him to roll off the edge of the bed and fall on the floor, ending up face down.

"Ah, you up," she said.

"Ughhh. You may notice, I'm actually on the floor"

"Like last night," she laughed. Ashley blinked now staring at the carpet, a mark left in his vision where the spotlight had temporarily blinded him. He struggled to pull himself back on the bed, lying sideways looking away from the ceiling lights. He noticed he was still in last night's clothes.

"Oh good god. I'm dead."

"Ha ha. You make sod of you." She'd picked this peculiarly

British term for idiot up and loved its simplicity and used it (wrongly) a lot. The last thing he wanted to hear is that his alcohol-fuelled (and thus not remembered) actions had been foolish and embarrassing the night before. The unknown possibilities struck fear into his heart.

"How do you know what happened?"

"You no see WhatsApp group?"

"I don't even know what fucking planet I'm on, let alone look at a group chat."

"Swear." Ashley couldn't be bothered apologising. She'd pointed out that his language had become bad since frequenting the club. The children had picked up on it, and they repeated 'fuck' at school to one of the teachers. "You check. It funny," she said and threw his phone on the bed. He couldn't move his eyelids so certainly wasn't going to move his body round to get his phone.

"You remember sicking?"

"Where did I do that?""

"Everywhere." Thais was enjoying this. Suddenly a memory came back of Budgie beside him whilst his head was down the loo. Oh Jesus "I warn you about brown spider."

"Yes yes. Can I get some paracetamol baby?" He unlocked his phone. There was red everywhere – missed calls, voicemails, text messages and WhatsApp notifications. This was going to be hell. The first one he opened was from David:

Quite a clean-up needed this morning. You might want to bring something in for Breeda. She was the one with the mop and disinfectant and used swear words I never knew even existed.

There wasn't one from the Irishwoman which indicated real anger. He suddenly seemed to have the numbers of the entire club, their family and friends.

One from Budgie:

Hope you're ok Ashley. Sore head I'd say though. It's Budge btw.

He noticed being added to the group 'Badcock post-match' by someone Ashley had no idea of. The group had over 100 members, male and female. He didn't recognise most names and wondered who they hell they were. The others were there though, Howley etc. The first post titled 'folks the owner.' Was the top one. It started shakily as someone approached Ashley and Budgie sitting down on the bar.

"How do you feel about the win boss?" the person behind the camera asked. Ahsley was looking down but when posed the question, his head lifted and rolled like a marble in cup with eyes that had long left the planet.

"I feel fucking fantastic," he slurred. Then it started, projectile vomiting. 'Eughhh' and cheers could be heard equally in the background. Budgie picked him by the back of his belt and scruff of his jacket. He held him like a dirty nappy and pointed Ashley away from himself. His size made Ashley look like a doll. It had clearly been shared with people outside the group. There were what seemed like thousands of emojis – the green puking one, the laughing smiley with tears and the pile of poo with eyes were the favourites. There were a lot of comments about people were so sad they missed it. He sweated like a fat man waiting for a burger whilst watching. He gave up looking at all the comments but now had a dilemma. Did he leave the group or stick it out to show he was resilient and it was all water off a duck's back. If he left, everyone would know and that, in his eyes, would show weakness. He decided to stick but mute it. Thais returned with tea and painkillers.

"You need get better, we round to Hans' for dinner tonight."

"Sorry love, can't, I'm having my balls nailed to a table."

Ashley eventually got out of his clothes, showered, turned his phone off, grabbed litres of water, berocca and paracetamol went to bed for the whole day. When the kids came back from their sleepover, Thais encouraged them to go wake daddy up. They applied themselves to their task admirably. Even a wet willie, something that would normally send Ashley into a rage (it was like torture to him) had no effect. All he could do was groan and pat away the little hands trying to irritate him.

It took Ashley three days to recover. After all the messages and general pisstake, he wasn't looking forward to going back to the club. On walking in to the bar, the first thing he needed to do was talk to Breeda. He'd bought flowers (the guilt ones), chocolates and had an envelope with £100 in. As usual, she sat at the bar on Facebook, or TikTok or whatever socials she used. She looked up and shot Ashley a stare that made his stomach churn.

"Breeda, I am so sorry." She didn't remove her gaze at the laptop, although she had clocked the flowers when Ashley was in the car park. She pretended to start typing something. "Breeda, you really are a superstar and I have no idea what this club would do without you." She stayed looking the screen but shrugged in agreement with Ashley's statement. "As a huge apology, I would love you to accept these," he said as thrust the ensemble her way. She looked at them and then him, shrugged and finally smiled as she grabbed the offering.

"You really shouldn't drink you know, it was like my granda's slurry spreader on the farm," she said.

"God do I know that. Listen, have you seen Budgie?"

"Not since the game, why?"

"Oh nothing, I just wanted to make sure I was all right with him."

"Oh, trust me, it would take a lot to get on his wrong side. He may look as though he'd rip your head off but he's a big softie really. You might want to buy him a new t-shirt though, the one from the other night, even Tyson wouldn't wear."

It was committee meeting time again and Ashley hadn't seen any of them since the party. He walked in to find them seated, looking like the smug cats that had found the cream factory.

"Ashley!" they all shouted in unison like they had rehearsed it. They had.

"Well well," David started it off. "We don't need to put any plastic sheets down do we?" Ashley knew he had to nip this in the bud.

"Right, let's get something straight. That wasn't my finest hour."

"Oh really," even Ritchie was chiming in.

"But I have apologised to Breeda and she's happy. I apologise to any of you if I insulted you or was just a dick. It has been done now and we will move on without any further mention thanks." It was just a chance for a bit of extracting the Michael for the committee but they'd seen he was clearly embarrassed about it, and after all, it was just a guy throwing up in front of everyone, so they decided to leave it.

24

Ashley thought after the great show the team put in for the semi, they needed to build on that spirit and bond further for what was ahead. In the corporate world, no organised team bonding event did what it was supposed to – enhance relationships between co-workers. Bosses like doing them because it shows their employees that they're really interested in the team's set-up. Attendees hate them because they usually eat into spare time where they could be doing something infinitely better than pretending to like Geoff from accounts. What the industry never grasps was that you either bond with a co-worker or you don't, simple.

This one was run by a university friend of Ashley's, Steve Lynagh. At uni he was known as stinky Steve on account of his horrendously smelly feet. His housemates made him put his trainers outside when they were taken off and not allowed in any way in to pollute their airspace. It had cost Steve many a date night. All guys wanted to do at college was drink and have sex. The education part only came when things got serious at the end. Lynagh decided to throw himself heartily into the drinking bit because he knew that if he ever got a girl back to his room–or hers– as soon as the trainers came off, so was she. When he made a bit of money and could afford private health insurance, he had them looked at and it turned out to be a medical condition caused by an overactive sweat glands in his feet.

The hotel where the retreat was held had originally been called the *Stoker's Rod* but was later changed to *Stokers Hall* as people got more sensitive to names. Ashley got a huge discount and didn't have to pay straight away because stinky owed him for handling a particularly unsavoury incident at the hotel. It was a group of government ministers and their staff. One of the ministers hadn't brought along a staff member but a prostitute. Because it was his away day from his wife and family, he took a packet of Viagra with him. His system reacted badly to the mix of large amounts of alcohol and the excessive amount of sildenafil citrate (the main ingredient of Viagra) resulting in him completely losing it. He ran out of his room, naked and standing to attention. He then ran through the bar doing what he called the helicopter where, without using any hands, he made his penis rotate like swinging a bit of string, and shouted 'helicopter time.'

The group of ministers and their staff could have sorted it internally and the public would be none the wiser. That was the plan until someone who worked there got hold of hotel CCTV showing the whole incident, not in black and white but full colour (it was an expensive system). They contacted Steve and told him they would release it to the press. Ashley managed to persuade the worker not to release the name of the hotel in return for an exclusive interview. He would secure the article aimed at launching the person's career as a minor celeb. He pulled the strings needed to get the interview done. They appeared on Love Island after that and embarked on an influencer career.

As the bus pulled into the hall with the team, it let out a big backfire bang which made Ashley wince slightly. He was sitting in the panelled bar being overlooked by large portraits of previous owners of the hall, dating back to when it was first built in the 1800s. The waiter looked a little startled by what sounded like an explosion and moved around to the window to see what had made the noise. Ashley didn't need look.

As the team and Shane decamped from the bus, to say the doorman was less than impressed would have been a mild understatement. Ashley greeted them in the grand reception where they looked like a rabble of prisoners on day-release. Apart, of course, from Fiona.

"Welcome all," Ashley beamed, "I have all your room keys

here."

The first exercise was the classic fall backwards trust one. The participant stands on a box with their back to six people lined up, three on each side, their arms linked. The person standing on the box then falls backwards without looking, expecting their fellow workers to break their fall. It was designed to foster trust between the faller and the catchers. The designer of the exercise didn't count on Badcock Town RFC. First up to put his trust in his teammates was the winger, Nowell. He was the live wire who'd always be first to try something out and to prank another teammate. He bounded up onto the box. The instructor for the proceedings was Stinky. He had devised the programme years before and, because Ashley was his mate, wanted to conduct the exercises himself. He told Nowell to fall backwards on the count of three. The catchers had all been pranked by the winger at some stage in their time and thought they'd take their own back. 1. 2. 3 Fall. They withdrew their clasped hands, leaving no net for Nowell. The body's natural instincts meant he managed to get a hand out, but it was still a very sore landing.

"What the fuck's wrong with you?" Howley shouted at them "That could have caused a serious injury, he could have broken his fucking neck." The guys were still laughing and as Ellis rose with no injury, he had to admit it was a good one. "Listen boys, take this seriously you hear now," Howley demanded. Although they wouldn't take a funeral seriously, the coach always commanded their respect. His words stopped the laughing and ensured the rest of the tasks would be at least tried in normal manner, that didn't mean they were successful though.

The paintball exercise was supposed to 'promote communication, trust, strategic planning, leadership, time & resource management, and flexible problem-solving.' All it really did was promote alpha macho egos with guns. The pattern of the paint on everyone after showed they all aimed for the groin area even though they were told expressly not to do that. Various other events didn't have the results aimed for. At the clay pigeon shoot, everyone dived for cover when Shambles turned around to talk to people, still pointing his loaded shotgun. The archery resulted in the unplanned death of a fox, the raft construction and racing resulted in an ambulance being called to treat hyperthermia.

Dinner was healthy, and the hotel were under strict instructions to limit the booze intake. This went down surprisingly well with the guys, with only a murmur of discontent. Afterwards Ashley and Fiona walked up the grand staircase towards the rooms.

"Why isn't Thais here?"

"Er, well, she had other plans."

"Did she know I was coming to this?"

"Well erm, ah."

"She doesn't right?"

"No."

"Why?"

"She wouldn't understand."

"Understand what?"

"This, you know me and you staying in a hotel."

"This is work, we're here with the team. I just don't get why she'd have a problem."

"She's a very jealous person."

"But she's got nothing to be jealous of."

"Oh yes, we know that, but you know, she can make an assumption out of the most innocent of things." They reached the corner in the hallway, her room was to the left, his to the right.

"Goodnight." Their heads mutually moved closer together in a pre-kiss routine. Ashley moved his mouth near hers, which then caused her to be startled as she flew back in reaction. She looked at him in horror and said goodnight as she retreated into her room and closed the door."

"Yes, yes. Goodnight Fiona." He got back to his room and once inside, started to kick his suitcase, bed and anything else within range.

"You stupid fucker Ashley," he remonstrated with himself.

"What did you do that for?" As much as he found her attractive, and he sure did, he never wanted to jeopardise what he had - his family. He muttered to himself about temptation and how it will always be out there for everyone but the key was not to give in to it. Deal with it and all will be ok. He eventually went to bed with a 'please can we turn back time' feeling about his person.

The next morning at breakfast, Ashley joined the table with Howley and Fiona. An awkward conversation about nothing took place between them all with Ashley and Fiona being reticent to get involved.

"You two all right?" the Welshman asked.

"Of course, just didn't sleep well." Ashley said.

"Well what do you think the boys got out of this?"

"Don't trust Shambles with a gun," Fiona said.

Before he lunged at her, Ashley was due to take Fiona back to London. That plan stayed but he was dreading it.

"So we need to talk right?" she said once they were off on their way.

"I am so sorry Fiona, I don't know what possessed me to do such a thing. I just hope we can forget about it and move on. I would hate that to do anything to our relationship and your being at the club."

"I do like you Ashley and I meant what I said, your wife's lucky to have you. But you know my history. I could never do that to another woman and family, no matter how attracted I was to the guy." Ashley was trying work out was that a good thing or not.

"Of course, it's not something I have thought about, just must have been the red wine. A moment of madness. I really am so sorry."

"I can forget a moment of madness," she said still looking sideways out of her window.

"And you'll stay at the club?"

"I'm not going to leave the lads at this stage."

"Oh thank God for that."

"But I reckon we should leave the social side of things between you and I, don't you."

25

The next day, Ashley spoke to Fortesque in the car on the way to the ground.

"Who'd have thought your shower of reprobates would meet my Spartans in the final," the booming toff said.

"I know right?"

"You do realise we'll murder you."

"Did you not see them in the semi. No Serge, and still won the semi. We can do it again. Beat your lot, don't you worry."

"I think you know deep down that was a one-off," Ashley half-heartedly protested. He did know that and didn't have faith that the team could reproduce that form to win. Bankruptcy loomed and although he had hope, he was a realist.

"Get out of the fucking way you moron!" Fortesque shouted. He too was in a car, displaying his roadside manner. "I have an offer for you Havers." The plan was outlined whereby Ashley would sabotage the team the day before the final. In return, he would get a percentage of the funds received from the developers once the land had been sold.

"Why would I do that?" Ashley asked.

"I know your plans once you get hold of it. You don't care about it, or the people there. So no matter what happens - you win or I win, it will end up a development."

"Those are my wife's plans."

"Still, face it Havers, it's a big gamble for you."

"What if we do win?"

"We both know the almost infinitesimal possibility of that happening."

"I need to talk to Thais about this."

It was date night at their local Italian, one of those rare restaurants that had been handed down three generations of family restauranteurs. Not normally that uncommon in other parts of Europe, but in London, there were only two or three such establishments – this was one of them. Wizardly old waiters oversaw the younger generation of keener family members. The service had its moments but the food had always been consistently amazing. Although date night had become less frequent as the years went on, it was still something Ashley enjoyed, even if their conversation had drifted from the belly-laughing dinners they used to have. They got on to plans about the club.

"Hans send surveyor. He say it good," Thais said as she tucked into her ossobuco.

"I don't think we can beat the Tans."

"Why?"

"We're still shit."

"Swear."

"Well we are. There's a chance we could do it, but a slim one."

"We no sell if lose?"

"Nope. Fortesque has offered me a deal though." Ashley outlined the plan that would provide for their children for close to the rest of lives.

"You do it."

"I don't know if I can."

"You sell anyway if win, what different?"

"I've grown attached to the club and the people."

"More than children?"

"Of course not."

"Simple then."

"Doesn't make me feel any better."

"You no kill no one."

"I do, believe me, I do."

Ashley walked through the club car park. It was foggy and wet with the perpetual UK drizzle that hung in the air telling anyone under it, they'd have it all day. Although not lashing down, it was the precipitation that soaked to the skin without seemingly getting the person wet. He'd composed the email to Mike Hunt many, many times. It had stayed in his 'drafts' folder for a week without him having the guts to push send. He looked out at the team training – it was back to normal. The intensity and image of pretending to be a real team had gone. Faf and Wilkinson were back to hating each other. The fullback was dropping balls again with deluded dad shouting from the sidelines. Howley shook his head whilst smoking as he shouted out players who were falling apart. Budgie grabbed Tiny by the shirt as they squared up to each other. On the scrum machine, when they snapped, the pack just collapsed into the mud without moving it a centimetre. Even Fiona wasn't there. Something Fortesque said hit was playing round and round in his mind. 'Do you really want to gamble your kids' inheritance on that shithole?'

Fortesque was wrong about one thing. Havers had grown fond of the club and everyone at it, even Shane. He took a sense of pride in what they'd achieved in the tournament and in his personal development in rugby. But when the deed was done, his children were guaranteed an awful lot of money. Plenty of school fees in there. So the landed gent was right about something, family always came first. He was working to provide his kids a future; all he did in a work perspective, was for them. He wanted to provide for them in an uncertain world that had the tendency to throw shit, no matter who you were. It wouldn't protect them from that but may help them deal with it.

He pulled out his phone, called up the draft email and stared at it for the hundredth time.

Dear Mike,

I have made a catastrophic mistake. Ellis Nowell, our wing, has been accepted into a club as a professional player. As such he was ineligible to play in our semi-final in the tournament. I am fully aware of the implications of this with regards to the final.

I would appreciate your confidentiality in this matter as I'm sure you'll be aware how hard this is going to be for me to tell everyone at the club, not least the players. I don't want anyone hearing it not from me.

Kind regards,

Ashley

A deep breath as his thumb hovered, then he hit send. A feeling akin to betraying a family member rushed over him in nauseating waves. A sense of loss greater than he ever imagined. Charlie and Harry were training with the minis, having a ball as ever. Fiona arrived beside him.

"This really means a lot to everyone you know." she said as they looked around at all the activity.

"I know," was all he could say looking at the ground, unable to look her in the eye.

"They're wonderful people, a bit rough around the edges some of them. You've given them this purpose and they could actually pull this off and save the club." Every single word caused the knife that had been rammed in his gut, to twist. 'Will this woman shut up, for the love of God' he thought as Hades engulfed his soul. He had to tell himself it was for the kids.

He got home in a terrible mood and argued with Thais about something completely trivial. The kids were excited about the game, and so pestered him with questions about tactics, plays and predictions as to how the final would go. They peppered their rat-a-tat-tat conversation with qualifications 'Budgie says' 'Howley says' etc. Ashley snapped at them to stop bothering him, something he immediately regretted. Over dinner, they had calmed down, as had their dad.

"Do you like playing rugby boys?"

"Of course daddy."

"What do you like about it?"

"Everything."

"Well can give me some things you like about it?"

"The game, playing with your mates in the mud, the feeling

you get when you score a try,"

"OK, what about the club, do you like that?"

"Oh yes."

"Why do you like it so much?"

"Budgie," they both said in unison. They thought more and then both listed off a whole load of reasons why they were Badcockians: Howley, winning (although Ashley was unsure where this came from, the minis had never won) and friends there.

"But you only play there on Sundays?" They played with their school teams on Saturdays so Sunday for Ashley wasn't given up to nice long lunches with copious amounts of wine. No, his Sundays were spent taking the kids to Badcock minis.

"It's way better than playing with the school. More real Daddy. Does that make sense?" It did, perfectly.

Whilst watching a movie (some nonsense about dragons) with the kiddos, he checked his phone and there was an email from Mike.

Dear Ashley,

Thank you for your email, I was very alarmed to read it.

Just to confirm, you fielded an ineligible player in your semi-final. If you confirm this, Badcock Town RFC will forfeit your place in the final with that taken by your opponents in the forfeited match. I just want to check this was the case before I do anything. Please confirm.

Kind regards,

Mike

The sickness, guilt and general bad feelings returned.

"What would you do if you couldn't play at Badcock?" he asked his kids.

"Oh no daddy, don't say that. That can't happen. We must play there." Ashley replied to Mike.

Dear Mike,

I'm so sorry to give you a heart attack. It seems I have made two mistakes in one day. I just had a call from Ellis. I thought he'd signed as a professional already, but no he hasn't. He will join them after the final when he'll sign a contract and embark on his professional career. So please disregard my earlier email, Nowell was perfectly eligible to play the semi and for that matter, the final too. No need for forfeit and we look forward to welcoming you to the ground on a great day. Please find attached an email from Ellis's soon-to-be director of rugby confirming this.

Ashley went out to the garden to call Fortesque.

"I can't do it," he said.

"You cowardly cat's prick, why the sudden change of heart?"

"The club's grown on me."

"You'll end up with nothing you lanky piece of shitstain."

"I'll have my integrity."

"Says the man going to sell it if you win."

"Again, we we'll see."

"No matter, I've got my own other insurance to make sure I get what I want. Mark my words Havers, you're fucked."

"Bring it on you fat bastard." Ashley felt a surge of testosterone. It had taken this many years to bring out the competitive male in him, the caveman.

"We'll fucking wipe the floor with you and your chav gang. Then you'll have nothing better to do than watch the fucking bulldozers take away your inheritance. You wanker." He cut off.

26

Ashley had a few of the worst nights' sleep in years leading up to final game day. Whilst his newfound camaraderie with the club had filled his heart, he managed to keep the elephant in the room hidden- the Havers' plans for the club after winning. The reason he could keep it at extreme arms' length was that: 1) he wasn't dealing with it, that was down to the wife and OCC, which meant it wasn't his problem, and 2) he'd confront it after the season ends and the club was (hopefully) in the black. For now he had other things to focus on.

When David came into the clubhouse, he met Fiona, carrying a box of the energy drinks towards the changing rooms. He wasn't expecting this but offered to lay them out for her.

"Just put them out beside the shirts, thanks David." A while went by.

"You fished those yet?" Fiona shouted from the corridor.

"Nearly, will be out in a sec."

"It's not that hard David. A blindfolded monkey could do it."

"Got distracted by a call."

"I need some help with the tackle bags if you could." These were another addition Howley brought in after being loaned by Gethin. The brothers had a pint a few days before and realised it was insane to bear grudge for such a minor thing. They still disagreed on who the GOAT was but this time, they just moved on to other matters, none more important than the upcoming Welsh home game against the English in the Six Nations finale. Nothing stirred the blood of a Welshman (or for that matter a Scotsman, Frenchman or Irishman) than the prospect of handing England a drubbing in front of their own supporters. It wasn't just tackle bags that Gethin loaned his brother. The scrum machine at Badcock had been left in a far flung part of the car park after one of the springs behind the pad, came through the foam and speared the no 1 like a harpoon. There were also a load of free weights and other various equipment pieces Badcock had never had. Shane got loaned a low loader from a friend and did the honours transporting all the equipment across the county.

Breeda's top had become even more revealing and her hair tousled as though she was going to a wedding. Ashley had learned that you have to fight fire with fire with her, there was no point in being a shrinking violet or you'd get mangled.

"Are you all right, has someone attacked you and dragged you through a hedge backwards?" Ashley had become at home with pisstaking.

"Ah go fuck yourself Bertie," she said without smiling. "And you can't take the piss out my clothes when Elton John has just arrived." Ritchie wore a new outfit. The coat was a bright red parker with a fur collar. No French ski instructor would have been seen dead in it. There was the obligatory Hawaiian shirt underneath and for some inexplicable reason, he'd resorted to coloured glasses al la Bono. He'd been to the hairdressers too, with an almost white bleach colour. His jeans were way to skinny for a man his age and his trainers looked like he's been painting with fluorescent paint in them.

"I hope you've got that PA system sorted," Ashley shouted

"All cool man," was the response.

"That fecker wouldn't know cool if it kicked him in the bollix."

"Zippy!" Bellowed Julian as he and Sarah arrived beside them.

"Zippy?" Breeda asked with a head tilted like a dog who hears its name.

"Oh it's nothing. Anyway how about this game?"

"You don't know the story?" Julian asked Breeda. When she shook her head, a stage was provided for the raconteur and he started in grand fashion. Ash moved off knowing that Julian was telling the worst possible person at the club about his mishap. Sarah grabbed his arm.

"You should have taken the deal Ash." She said softly tinted with a hint of menace.

Havers caught up with Howley, who looked like he'd been dragged backwards through a hedge. His bloodshot eyes were underlined by deep black bags. The Welsh top had been washed though and a cigarette hung out the corner of his mouth.

"Have a few beers last night?" Ashley asked.

"Couldn't sleep, not a wink."

"Run out of fags?"

"It's this bloody game, the tourney, the whole shooting match boyo."

"Hold on, the great Howley Davies is stressed." Howley fixed Ashley with a steely, slightly crazed look.

"We had an interesting visitor yesterday."

"Oh yes, Martin Johnson?" Ashley was proud of another unsolicited rugby reference.

"A surveyor."

"That fat fucker Fortesque! Can't leave us alone. Wants to rub it in"

"That's what Shane thought as he kicked him off the premises."

"Now I feel sorry for the guy."

"As Tarface gave him a bit of dig, he said he'd no idea who Fortesque was, he was there as instructed by the Havers." It suddenly dawned on Ashley, he'd dealt with their plans by staying well out of it. Now the worst person to encounter a surveyor had extracted information by torture.

"So, I can explain Howley." Out of the corner of his eye, Ashley saw a flash of red. It was Howley showing a turn of speed and agility that hitherto had been beyond him in his later years. His face matched the colour of his shirt. It was filled with rage. His right hook caught Ashley square on the chin. He went down face down in the mud. He'd never been punched in the face before, and boy did it hurt.

"You've broken my jaw you madman," Ashley said whilst struggling to his feet out of the mud. Howley hadn't.

"You were going to sell it all along right?" The realisation that Howley knew, hit him harder than the Welshman had.

"It's more complicated than that Howley," Havers said as he got back up.

"This tournament has given me something that stops me jumping under a bus. The idea of being here next season, playing, winning, tournaments, the lot. These boys, the club, Jockey. I want to win this fucking thing and build the place to be an essential part of the community. Getting through this game is all that matters right now, not just to me but all of us. No point in bothering the boys right now with what a complete fucking arsehole you are. I have to get these lads through this and the last thing they need is dealing with that. So we'll continue on as normal right?" Ashley nodded. "But afterwards, you and I have serious unfinished business," he said pointing a menacing finger at Ashley who was rubbing his chin. There was dragon fire in his blue eyes.

Then the team started turning up, early for them. They looked serious, more serious than ever. They still had some jokes, mainly at Ritchie's expense, but they did look as though they were thinking about the game. They were. All knew about the club's predicament. Although before no-one ever gave a monkey's about the running of the club nor winning for that matter, they had been on this journey knowing that if they don't win, BTRFC would be no more. The guys were their mates. Rugby was the thing that bound them all together, even if that meant always losing. It was an escape for some. It was the sense camaraderie, all in it together. That had only intensified as they progressed in the tournament. It was true that Nowell had been offered a pro contract but he told them he couldn't join the team until the final was over. He, like Serge, had the desire to do it for the boys. Faf was grappling with all sorts of rugby playing demons. Not good enough for the Boks and his mind being tortured by the effects of the steroids. But nothing mattered more in rugby than this moment, the boys, the club. The whole place was all Budgie had. An only child and with his parent long gone, they were his family, full stop. So they all had motivations and reasons to make sure that they played well above their actual talent and get the job done, for everyone.

Ashley and Howley watched the warm-up along with a hefty crowd. Ashley kept rubbing his chin and looking over at Howley who just shook his head. Ashley couldn't blame Howley for lamping him. They were both going to get through the game and then deal with everything afterwards. The game was the important thing, the rest could wait. The guys were hitting the tackle bags with gusto. Fiona with the whistle got them to do jogs, sprints, press-ups, resistance bands and stretches.

"Dusty's going to do it for you here. Then I reckon England will be calling up. You won't mind if he has to move on to the pros and internationals." Delusional dad said after approaching the pair.

"I truly hope he achieves all he can and if that is with England and elsewhere, he will have our full support," Ashley said. Dad didn't know how to respond so just nodded and moved off.

Supporters from both sets had been arriving in dribs and drabs, but with an hour to kick off, the ground was full, or as full as it could be. The outside bar was doing a raging trade as Ritchie played some nice tunes at normal sound levels. Kids were messing about with rugby balls bigger than them.

Thais arrived with Charlie and Harry. They immediately ran off towards the sideline where Budgie was warming up. They shouted over and he gave them a big thumbs up.

"Mike," Ashley greeted the owner of Hunt Sewage.

"Quite a thing with Sella, shame he had to go back."

"His dad's fine and recovering at home but Serge still needs to be there."

"Well at least I met him."

"Indeed."

"So glad that was a mistake about your winger. I'm rooting for you guys. You've livened this tournament up like never before."

"That's very kind Mike."

"Plus, I really can't stand that fucker Fortesque.

"Seems like you're not alone."

"What do you reckon, your lot going to do it?"

"They're up for it, so let's see."

"Good luck, have a good match."

Howley stood in the middle of a fully changed and ready to go 1st XV BTRFC, all seated on the benches under lockers around in a square. They faced the coach with intense concentration. The Wales top had been replaced with a Badcock shirt underneath a generic trackie top. He sparked and crackled as if attached to the mains. This fed into the atmosphere the guys were feeling. Fiona stood in a corner with a towel round her neck and holding water bottles. Ashley had been banned. As per the superstitions, the team thought because they had won when he didn't go in before a game, he shouldn't ever again, bad luck.

"Here we are boys. Somewhere no-one would have given us a chance to be. But we're fucking here right! Win this, we keep the club, fucking simple." His Richard Burton, soft-toned voice was now gritty, powerful and laced with menace. "Be first to every breakdown. Make every tackle count. In the scrum, front up boys, drive those guys into the ground. Take that spirit we had from the semi and fucking double it, treble it. Hit them as hard as you've ever hit anything before. Don't take a step backwards. Make sure those fuckers know who we are."

The team all stood up and put their arms over the shoulders of players next to them in a huddle. Faf joined Howley in the middle and started shouting.

"Fucking do it for the club yah."

"Whoaaaa!" they all shouted.

"Do it for Jockey."

"Whoaaaa!"

"Do it for the boys you're going into battle with."

"Whoaaaa!"

"The boys stood beside you right fucking now."

"Whoaaaa,"

"Look around boys. Do it for each other."
"BADCOCK! BADCOCK GO!!! HUHHHH!"

27

Everyone waited for the teams to emerge from the clubhouse. Over the PA, Ritchie introduced the Spartans. From the cheers, it seemed half the crowd were Spans, as they were known. Then BTRFC were introduced, and the cheers were louder and more raucous than anyone could ever remember. The noise possibly helped because they'd all been drinking for longer after arriving earlier. Howley joined Ashley, Thais, and Fiona, standing on the side by the halfway line.

Pre-match rituals completed, and they were off. Just as many hotly-anticipated games usually did, this one failed to live up to the billing for the first 15 minutes. There was plenty of grunt, endeavour and kick tennis. Although no great skill or line breaks were in evidence, it was clear to everyone watching that the Tans looked way more dangerous than Town. They were putting together moves that would have torn the defence to shreds if they had come off. But they kept dropping passes. Plus BT were doing well at slowing the ruck ball down. Faf made a nuisance of himself, trying to wind up every Spartan player that came within a few feet of him. He chirped, niggled, sledged, and generally irritated like a wasp at a picnic on a sunny day.

Badcock Town 3 Spartans 0

Shane wandered up and stood beside Ashley. He had a non-regulation can of super strong lager that wasn't being sold at the bar. No one bothered asking him.

"Awight."

"Hi Shane, close game."

"Yeah."

"Think we can do it?"

"Fucking better do, I've got a grand on them." He said, using more words than hitherto previously managed.

"You can bet on a game like this?"

"If you know the right people, you can bet on which hooker has the clap."

"Lovely."

Fortesque sent Ashley a text from his position further down the touchline:

When we get it going, you guys are fucked. Don't look like the team from the semi to me.

Ashley looked over to him down the pitch who waved a fat hand at him forcing Havers to sneer. The pompous ass was right though, this was nothing like the performance from that game. A Span player went down resulting in a huddle of the Town players around Faf. No one could hear what he was shouting, but it was clearly a bollocking. Whatever he said, worked. The next thirty minutes were the best BT had played in its 200-year history. Serge didn't count because that was just a one-man show, this was a team effort. Better at the breakdown, instead of slowing it, they were winning it. They were more aggressive and crucially, more clinical in what TV folk like to call the red zone, the space between the 22-yard and try lines. They scored two converted tries, and Wilkinson kicked a couple of pens. Even Shambles was hitting his marks, and Dusty put in a fine performance under the high ball. The Spartans couldn't believe it, they'd always known this team as less than useless, but they were being beaten. Howley and Faf had inspired the lads to play as though they were a couple of leagues above their skillset.

HT - Badcock Town 23 Spartans 6

They got a huge roar from every Town supporter in the place when they trouped off to the huts for halftime. Plenty of backslapping. Faf went along the line, screaming at each player as if they'd just won the match. He was one of those players that would infuriate the opposition for being 'that annoying little shit'. For those on his side, he was giving them a focal point for their aggression and a rallying call to follow. Ashley followed Howley and Fiona along the sideline on his way back into the clubhouse.

"That was incredible, I'm very proud of the boys," he proclaimed. Howley just nodded, still seething.

"We still got 40 minutes to fuck it up though," a wag by the bar said as they overheard the remark. Ashley caught Fortesque's eye when they passed. Havers smiled at him from ear to ear, making the blood rush to the landowner's face in a fit of anger, who stormed off where David intercepted him. Ritchie fired up the music (modern dance, not old stuff) on the PA, and everyone was having a party.

The teams' return portrayed very different pictures. Spans ran out onto the pitch like raging bulls. They looked chastened but angry, like they wanted to rip peoples' heads off. The coach had clearly given them the hairdryer treatment. Then Town ran out looking ever so pleased with themselves. They lapped up the cheers from the crowd and waved to family, friends and partners providing the cheers. Immediately there was something wrong. No Faf. In his place was Austin Youngs, a 19-year-old who had shown promise in the 2nds but would never have shifted Faf off the starting no9 spot in normal circumstances. He was known as SpongeBob from his schooldays when his mum used to iron his underpants, making them look square. Howley and Fiona followed the team.

"Where's Faf?" Ashley asked. The physio and coach both shook their heads as if something horrific had happened.

"He fucking exploded, never seen anything like it," Howley said.

"He's got a bad tummy problem, really, really bad," Fiona said as she moved off, shaking her head.

"Is that us done Howley?" Again, he was ignored.

The second half began with Spartans receiving the kick off

and putting a well-practised move into play. The second row who caught the kick, went into the routine with his fellow forwards where it looked like they were going into a ruck. The outcome would normally be to do the spider legs at the back of the ruck, thus allowing the scrum half to carry out the textbook clearing kick. But instead of taking the ball into the tackle, he did a sidestep Campese would have been proud of. The forwards around him were expecting this and suddenly created a short line across the gain line rather than back away from it. The effect took out most of the Town chasers who were also expecting normal play. The ball was moved skilfully through the pack's hands, pulling in all the defenders. It left a four-on-two out wide for the speed merchants, who duly obliged and added the bonus of cutting across to go under the posts. All town supporters suddenly feared for the worst, a usual performance resulting in a hammering.

Badcock Town 23 Spartans 13

On the following restart, the Tans tried another fancy move, but Budgie had been wise to it this time. All the training with Fiona had paid off as his upper body strength and muscle tone had increased in a way that some of the guys joked that he'd been on Faf's pills. He did something no one who played with him had ever seen: the jackal. He won a penalty to the delight of his comrades. However, Town missed touch, allowing Tans to exit. Although they'd managed to mess it up, that steal stopped their heads going down and refused to accept a drubbing was on the horizon.

Ashley looked down at his kids going ballistic on the sideline, shouting, 'Come on Town! Come on Town!' Wilkinson gathered the team around in another huddle. The crowd could hear him shouting instructions and encouragement with quite a bit of swearing, then silence. They then saw the huddle part suddenly and Wilkinson run with his hand to his mouth back to the clubhouse. Fiona ran after him, emerging almost immediately.

"He's got it too, what the fuck's going on?" she said to Howley and Ashley.

"Fuck!" shouted the coach. "Get young Bernard on," Howley instructed. The young number 10 was called that because he used to work on a Turkey farm where his job was to inseminate the females with sperm from a syringe. His surname was Matthews, so of course he got called Bernard by everyone, even though his first name was Philip. "Now we really are screwed," the Welshman said.

The tournament rules meant that each team could only have two substitutes on the bench. Again, the organisers thought this more competitive and exciting than endless troops of 'bomb squads' or 'finishers'. If a player was substituted, they could not return to the field. Only players that had been registered with Hunt Sewage pre-game could come on. So Town had no subs left and couldn't replace anyone if needed as there was no one left.

Badcock Town 23 Spartans 27

Two more converted tries for the Spartans, and with fifteen minutes to go, Town had another injury with a knock to the head, which meant they would have to play the last period with only 14. Then Dusty had to run to the toilet, joining the others with an upset stomach. Town down to 13 men, with a penalty and a kick to touch by the 22. More calamity - Nowell twisted his ankle. Town down to 12.

28

Ashley, Howley and Fiona, stood on the touchline. Beside them, seated looking almost transparent, were Faf, Wilkinson and Robinson. The three players could not cheer, stand up, shout or commit any exertion without risking having to run off again. Nowell had an ice pack wrapped around his ankle.

"If you can't bring on at least one more player, you'll have to forfeit the game," the ref told them.

"That's ridiculous sir," Howley said. "Teams can play with ten if they have to."

"Not in this tournament, I'm afraid, 13 is the minimum."

"Jesus fucking Christ!" Howley shouted.

"I'll give you a couple of minutes. Surely you've got another registered payer here?"

"I'm a registered player," Ashley proffered. They all stared at him motionlessly. Faf tried to exaggerate laugh out loud and stopped immediately with a surprised face, fearing the consequences. He might have gone too far too soon. Fiona picked up the laughter at the proposition of Ashley a player. "Trust me, I am registered. The ref can ask Mike Hunt himself." When Ash registered Sella for the tourney, he also did himself. He wasn't planning on playing but thought it would give him kudos at the club if he showed willing to get stuck in. He never in his wildest dreams expected to actually play though. "There's one play left right?" the group nodded. "Well surely you can come up with one that involves me." They all looked around unsure. "Look at me, when I run on, no one, I mean no one, is going to be convinced that I can turn it around. They'll take their eye off me, which is something we can exploit no?" They all continued to look back and forth at each other trying to process the info Ash had just imparted.

"We'll do French toast," Howley said.

"That could work," Faf managed to say. Wilkinson agreed.

"Gather the lads here Fiona." It was a play designed for the semi when Sella was a Badcockian, but they never got to use it. It was simple enough. When they had a scrum anywhere near the opposing 22 left side, quick ball would mean Faf kick cross field to the wing. With a successful chase, over Nowell would go relatively unopposed. For it to work, the space needed to be out wide with a 2 plus 1 for the attackers. This was created with Serge acting as 10 running a dummy run down the middle so that all the defenders focussed on him.

Havers ran to the lost property box in the clubhouse. The only shorts in there looked like they'd been misplaced by one of the minis. They left nothing to the imagination as he jogged over.

"Oh dear God, at least we know he's been circumcised now. Jaysus," Breeda remarked.

"What you do?" Thais asked him as he jogged past.

"I can't let them down. I need to make this right." He joined the huddle around Howley.

"Right lads, last play. Let's make it fucking count right," Davies shouted.

"You can do it boys. For the glory. For each other!" Faf shouted as loud as he could from the touchline. They all screamed the club shout and broke. Howley stopped Ashley.

"You know what you're doing right?"

"Got it coach."

"And try to look more pathetic than you actually do when you run over to your position."

"That won't be a problem."

"Take the far right-hand side. You need to have your eyes glued to SpongeBob. Stay level with him before the kick at all costs."

"What happens if I don't?"

"Offside. Penalty to them. We lose, you lose, the club loses. Shane might even put a contract out on you." Ash was under no doubt about the importance of staying onside. "Then when he does kick, assuming you stay in those shorts, run like hell. If he gets it right, the ball will come to rest in the corner goal area with only you bearing down it. When you go to ground, make sure you're in control. Use both hands outstretched in front of you"

Mike was called over and had to confirm the owner was indeed registered for the tourney and legit. Ashley ran on to universal laughter and mocking from Spartans. The tight shorts were a particular source of pisstake. He took Howley's advice to heart and purposefully tripped over his own feet, to more hilarity. Then budgie shouted to the team as loud as he could, with the sole intention of getting it in the Tans' mind.

"All out down the middle lads. Everyone all in. Our time to score that fucking try!" he said as he gestured for all the backs to bunch up in a group right behind SpongeBob. "Let's smash them!" As they manoeuvred, no Spartan noticed Ash hadn't. He was an insignificant part of a well-advertised move straight at the heart of the defence. First part of the plan achieved, now they just had to win it, and the South African do the biz. Before the whistle went to start, Ash thought he might start hyperventilating. He remembered his therapist's coping mechanism for this. It involved squeezing his hands and focusing on calm things that made him happy. He couldn't do that distracting tactic here, the thing he needed to focus no here was staying behind SpongeBob and then run like hell. 'Fuck that hand technique' he thought.

The forwards packed down, his heart was going a million bpm. He looked around the ground. The cheering crowd, the staff, the players, he was proud of the place. Scrum collapse and reset. Another collapse with the ref warning there would be a penalty to Spartans if it happened again. Budgie brought the forwards into a huddle and some gentle words that mainly involved fuck and fucking. Down they went again, a slight wheel but stayed up. The ball came to the number 9 quickly at the base. Youngs then showed why people had mentioned him being a possible England international one day. The packed midfield on the right, started their runs as if they were going straight. The defenders all were drawn into them. SpongeBob moved right and feigned to pass to them but then, with a magical touch, went left back around the back of the breaking-up scrum, veered right and put in the kick off the outside of his right boot (later described as a worldie - by him). Just Ash needed now.

When Havers saw the ball hit the scrum-half's boot, he launched himself like a sprinter. His shorts caught his testicles awkwardly, creating pain something akin to being kicked in them. It caused a slight wobble in the legs, and this would normally have floored him, but this time he had to keep going. Nothing was going to stop him. He was possessed, one thing on his mind, making amends. He saw the ball in the air out of the corner of his eyes, he was just focusing on the straight ahead– where there was no-one in front of him. He aimed for the spot he was told the ball would be. His target area was honing into view. He could still the hear the crowd shouting and cheering but hat made no difference. As he reached the tryline, there was grass still in front of him. A Gilbert suddenly appeared. It landed in a way like it was landing in water. It stopped dead. There it was. He had to get here for everyone, for everything. He was aware of a Spartan running towards him but they were to the side. The rest was a blur.

29

It was the summer party at BTRFC, and did they have something to celebrate, not least winning the Hunt Sewage tournament. Ashley had only ever seen the ground in the cold and wet. Now the grass was the colour it was supposed to be, i.e. not brown. The trees were full and lush, and even the 60s clubhouse sparkled in the sunshine. He stood at one end of the outdoor bar that had stayed in place since the final. According to Shane, the people he got it off, didn't want it back. He observed everyone with a sense of looking on at his own family. There were plenty of tables set up so people could sit down as they consumed dangerously undercooked chicken legs, sausages and burgers from the BBQ. Ritchie was doing the tunes, still with the signature DJ moves. However, gone were the ridiculous clothes. He was dressed in a black t-shirt and jeans. Gone too was the remains of his hair having given up the pretence that he still had any. He'd clearly not accounted for the sun on skin that had never seen the sun before and was very badly sunburnt. He looked like a cherry tomato. Dusty came over.

"I want to apologise for my dad."

"Don't worry about it, he's part of the furniture."

"He can be a real pain. I know I'm a shit player really, but he thinks I'm not."

"He's just being a proud dad, as any father would."

"I do love playing rugby. I love playing here with these boys. It means the world to me. So thank you." Dusty departed, caught up with Steve and put his arm round his old man as they walked off.

One notable absentee from the festivities was David. He'd been exposed as Fortesque's spy. He was also the Spartan owner's secret weapon on the final day. Raging with anger that he hadn't received the club, or at least a share of it, he did a deal with Fortesque for a few hundred grand. On the morning of the final (and nearly rumbled by Fiona) he injected the three main players' energy drinks with a drug used for veterinary surgery. He'd been given the dose by Sarah who was also in cahoots with Smythe. She got the drug from the vet that tended her horses on the farm. It was normally given to animals before gastric surgery and basically cleared the system out. David had been found out by Breeda via something only she and Woody knew about. The useless handyman had once made an attempt to install air conditioning. The sum of his efforts was a hole in the boardroom floor (covered by a grate) that led down to the pantry off the kitchen. It did have its uses because that's how Breeda could hear every word said in the boardroom. It's why committee members could hear her voice in a ghostly fashion echo around the place. At halftime in the final, she nipped into the pantry to get some more burger buns and heard David and Fortesque talking.

"Did you do it?" asked the landowner.

"Yes. I did."

"Then why aren't they fucking collapsing with stomach cramps?"

"I don't know, I put it in as instructed, they should be."

"It better work or else you get nothing."

"I can't tell you how much it's hurting and how much I think you're a complete wanker."

"You'll get over it when you see the money. It's funny," he paused for effect. "People always do when they see a figure with noughts on."

"You're wealthy enough, why do you do this?"

"I have to win. Whether it's a property deal, golf or guessing which cow is going to have shit, I cant stand to lose."

When Breeda told Howley just before the second half, she was instructed to get Shane to see David off the premises. Apparently, there had been the odd dig to his ribs from mullet man as he did so. The last anyone heard, David was running a Royal British Legion club somewhere up north.

Howley joined Ash. They both looked over to one of the tables on the edge. Thais was one side writing something in a notebook. Opposite her were Budgie and Breeda. He looked like someone was explaining the prime theories in quantum physics. She had a face of thunder, arms crossed. Charlie, Harry and some boys and girls were chucking a ball around nearby.

"I think Breeda is regretting asking Thais to be her wedding planner," Ash said.

"Budgie's thinking what the fuck have I got myself into here."

"Thais wants understated chic. Breeda wants princess pink from Neverland."

"We know who's going to win.

"Howley, I want to build something for the community here, something they can be proud of, something that will bring them together like never before. Increased membership, boys, mini rugby, under 16s, girls, women, the lot." Ashley said.

"Quite the visionary. What changed?"

"The club, it gets to you. The ethos, the people, the game. I can see where Jockey was coming from"

"Finally."

"I've grown to love the club, its members, the staff and even you Howley."

"Don't cry now boyo."

"And I'm so glad you'll be with me." They clinked glasses.

"Have you asked Shane to leave?" the coach asked.

"I've actually given him a permanent spot in the car park." Howley shot him a surprised look. "Well it's good luck right."

Serge's dad made a full recovery, and Badcock arranged the inaugural tour to Bayonne. They had to organise passports for some of the team who'd never been out of the county, let alone the country. It became an annual event. Serge went back to international rugby, going on to become the most capped French player of all time. Seeing the kids loving mucking about on

Serge's farm, Ash and the family never went back to Mykonos. They bought a run-down farmhouse in Bayonne, where they spent every school holiday.

Faf went back to South Africa to own and run a gym named *Muscle Madness.* SpongeBob became a very successful England international, winning a world cup. Wilkinson made a fortune selling his software company and stayed at the club with no particular honours apart from being their best player. Nowell became a pro after the final and played for Smitherwick for decades until he put his back out with the vets' team.

Fortesque swore revenge.

Ashley found himself alone in the bar as everyone partied outside. Fiona, who couldn't make the bash because she had to go abroad for work, rang.

"I really hope you'll stay?" Ashley said.

"I've had more fun doing this than anything ever before."

"I've got money and plans. I want you to our fitness director."

"Well.."

"And I want you to create a women's team. Get the girls into rugby and be successful as a club and team. Perhaps we can feed into the England side, who knows?"

"Let's see Ash."

He put the phone down and glanced out the window to see Budgie holding a ball in a sizeable hand above the kids who were jumping up trying to grab it. Thais laughed and clapped as she watched. He looked at the walls which had plenty of new pictures, mainly featuring the shit tournament trophy held by various people. Then there was the one of him going over the line to score. It was in a frame beside a picture of Jockey. He was snapped mid-air, arms outstretched, a ball on the ground in front of him. One of his legs was higher than the other in a scissors-type pose. The devil was in the detail. Upon closer inspection of the photo, a testicle and the top of his penis had escaped the minuscule shorts. He protested at its display, but everyone told him it was the only picture anyone had of the most famous try in the history of Badcock Town RFC. Of course it wasn't. He smiled in recognition.

"A Badcockian all right."

THE END

I can't tell you how grateful I am that you made it to the end and invested your valuable time in reading my nonsense. I really hope I put a smile on your face at some stage. If you did enjoy this, I would really appreciate a rating or review.

My next one is set in the football world.

BOOKS BY THIS AUTHOR

Boo's Last Shot

A funny tale about about a golf pro's comeback.

The stakes are higher than ever for Boomer (aka Boo), a superstar coming out of retirement for one last shot at his dream prize - the Masters.

Death Of A Rock Star

Murder mystery comedy. Agatha Christie meets Monty Python.

The clock is ticking for a hapless PI to prove it was murder and not an accident.

Printed in Great Britain
by Amazon

28640431R00089